The Spirit of Christmas

Lauraine Henderson

ISBN-10: 1983489530
ISBN-13: 978-1983489532

DEDICATION

This book is dedicated to everyone who loves the classics of Christmas, but always wants a good romance, too!

ACKNOWLEDGMENTS

I am grateful to Mr. Charles Dickens, and his inspiring classic, *A Christmas Carol.* It is one of my favorite stories of the holidays, in every adaptation.

I would like to thank my devoted beta readers for their encouragement and for taking the time from their busy lives to help me see the story with fresh eyes.

A special thanks to my editor, Sandra Meaders, for finding all the little holes in my plot and helping me refine the details I couldn't see on my own.

As always, thanks to my wonderful family for their support and indulgence.

And last, but not least, thanks to my Heavenly Father who inspires me daily and helps me bring my thoughts to life.

1

Stone and McAllister. The faded lettering on the double-glass doors had started to disappear, showing its age, but George Stone didn't want to spend the high cost of new lettering. Geoff McAllister may be dead and gone, but it didn't change George's business or his plans.

A slight fluttering slithered down George's spine when he thought of Geoff's untimely death. No one that young should have a massive heart attack. It shocked the software community. Yet, within only days, Geoff's death was old news and life, well, business, went on.

George pushed through the building entrance and walked boldly through a small reception area toward his office. As he hung his worn woolen coat on the coat hook just inside his office, he walked to the employees' staff room and poured himself a tall glass of water. Taking the glass back to his desk, he settled into the chair his grandfather had used for his own business, turned on his computer, and pulled up his email to start his day.

Promptly at 7:50 am, George's executive assistant, Kathryn Gleason, breezed through the reception room and poked her head into George's office.

"Good morning, Mr. Stone," Kathryn's bubbly voice danced

into the room and George tried to hide his cringe. She was such a morning person. Of course, he wasn't much different from morning to evening, so there wasn't much of a comparison.

"Morning," was all the effort he mustered.

Instantly, the bubbly voice and smile were gone, but she couldn't hide her beauty. It was the only thing George didn't like about Kathryn. She was certainly competent at her job and she got along well with the other employees which allowed him to avoid them as much as possible. Her only fault, which he admitted most people wouldn't consider a fault, was that she was too pretty. Some might even say she was beautiful. It was distracting at times and George berated himself whenever he started thinking about her beauty rather than her job performance.

George heard her humming a tune while she opened her computer. He got up and closed his office door. He never did like her humming, either.

Kathryn Gleason sighed as the door to Mr. Stone's office swiftly closed. She had done it again. It wasn't like she tried to offend him, but it didn't seem to matter if she was her usual friendly self or just professionally polite, he always closed the door as soon as she came to work. If she thought too hard about it, she would think he didn't like her, but he treated everyone the same way, some people much worse, so she didn't take it too personally.

Within minutes, employees slowly trickled into the office and computers started buzzing. By the time Kathryn had responded to several new emails and gone through the snail mail, it was time for their weekly staff meeting. She grabbed the selection of coffees, teas, and hot chocolate she brought from home. Mr. Stone may not approve of providing beverages for the weekly staff meeting, but she wouldn't let that stop her. Everyone worked hard and in these tough economic times, they were all lucky to have a job. The business was doing well and Kathryn didn't understand why Mr. Stone was so stingy.

After placing the instant beverage packets on the back table next to the microwave—their one luxury in the staff room—Kathryn stood at the door and greeted everyone who entered with her usual cheerful smile. When Mr. Stone arrived, promptly at 10:00 am, her smile was still in place. But his handsome face, while not exactly scowling, wasn't even near a pleasant expression and it saddened Kathryn's heart. Here was a man who had it all. He was tall, handsome, and extremely successful. His chiseled jaw and raven black hair were swoon-worthy until he opened his mouth. He even lived in a big old house, but he wore a perpetual frown.

Dedicated to his company, she never took a call from anyone other than clients or suppliers and he never made a call in her hearing to anyone other than those same business contacts. The only exception was the occasional drop-in visit from his nephew, James. Kathryn had a hard time putting the two of them together. Mr. Stone was all that was serious and dreary and James, all that was fun and cheerful.

Mr. Stone began the meeting. "Thank you all for being here on time. We will address any old business first. Kathryn…"

"Yes, of course." Kathryn, momentarily lost in her thoughts, quickly regrouped and presented the minutes from last week's meeting and took additional notes as the weekly topics were reviewed. When new business was opened to the room, all eyes turned to Kathryn.

With a half-smile and quick swallow, Kathryn turned to Mr. Stone and looked directly at his big, dark brown eyes. He looked back at her with a stare that could win contests.

But Kathryn wasn't going to back down. Especially when she had thoroughly convinced herself most of Mr. Stone's gruff exterior was simply a front for an unhappy man.

"Yes, well," she began, "the staff has unanimously requested an instant coffee machine and hot water dispenser for the staff room. We looked into the costs and we can get a used model from a local coffee company for half the price of a new one and they would be willing to sell us the coffee with only a 10% markup. It's really a great deal."

George Stone's stare was turning into a glare. "Again?"

"Well, we thought you might consider it if you realized what a great savings we were going to get." She wore her most encouraging smile.

"Cute," he remarked. "Save it for the clients, Ms. Gleason. I'm sorry, everyone, we don't have the budget for complementary coffee and tea in this office. If it's that important to you, you are welcome to look for work elsewhere." It was the same speech every week. He wasn't even wearing down. As he stood to end the meeting, he gave Kathryn that look; that look that said he was disappointed in such a subject being brought up yet again. Kathryn cast her eyes down to her lap and resisted the grin that threatened to mock his glare. What he really needed, she decided was some Christmas spirit. But Christmas was still a week away. The office staff still had that hurdle to overcome and she would be on vacation. Fortunately, Christmas landed on a Sunday this year and her gratitude knew no bounds. It meant everyone would have Christmas Eve and Christmas off and he could be grumpy by himself all weekend.

As Mr. Stone made his way back to his office and promptly closed the door, several staff members gathered around Kathryn to commiserate about him taking frugality to the limit. But it wasn't in her to gossip or complain.

"Guys, just leave it be and be grateful we have the weekend for Christmas this year."

Agreeable murmurings followed her back to her desk and she resumed her work for the morning.

2

"Hello and Merry Christmas, Kathryn," the pleasant voice offered the cheerful greeting as an attractive young man walked boldly through the double doors.

"Well, James, it's so nice to see you. Merry Christmas to you, too. Are you here to have lunch with your uncle?"

James's laugh sounded so foreign in the little office, several heads looked up from their respective desks.

Kathryn's smile couldn't be hidden. "I'll just let him know you're here."

James soft smile on his handsome face gave Kathryn a glimpse of what his uncle might look like if Mr. Stone ever allowed such a thing to break his face. She sighed. If only.

A quick knock on the door, a crisp call to enter, and James disappeared inside the den of the gloomy man. The door didn't close all the way and Kathryn had a perfect view of the inner office interactions.

"Hello, Uncle George. Merry Christmas!"

George looked up from his desk and did scowl this time. "Don't you have work to do?"

"I'm experiencing a wonderful invention that is actually enforced by law."

"Whatever are you talking about?"

"I'm on my lunch hour."

"You get an entire hour?"

"I know that would seem a waste of 45 minutes to you, but there you are. I get an entire hour and with that time, I've come to invite you to spend Christmas day with Jenny and me. Dad's coming, too."

"I can't believe you're married. You aren't even twenty-one yet."

"Hey, when you meet the right girl, why wait?"

"What a waste of youth."

Kathryn got up and closed the door the rest of the way.

George took note of the door closing and kept his thoughts to himself. He wasn't exactly averse to marriage, it just wasn't for him. He couldn't see how it would pay. "Thanks for the invitation, but no thanks."

"I was pretty sure you would say that, but if you ever decide to change your mind, just stop by. You're always welcome."

"I'm sure you have better things to do than stand here and invite me to a dinner you know I won't come to."

A tentative knock sounded on his office door. "Come in," he ordered.

Kathryn was usually bold and friendly. Now she seemed a little cautious. "Um, there's someone to see you," she said in a loud whisper. "He said it couldn't wait."

"Who is it?"

Before Kathryn could answer, a tall, plump, older man sporting a shock of white hair and a white beard burst into the room with a jubilant smile taking up his entire face and a brilliant light in his eyes. "Mr. Stone? Just the man I need to see!"

George eyed the bombastic man warily. "Who are you, sir?"

"Christopher Hardy is my name. I represent a conglomeration of non-profit organizations and we are going door to door this year in search of businesses to help the needy."

George sniffed as though Mr. Hardy had walked through a neglected dog park. James smiled and patted Mr. Hardy on the back.

"Mr. Stone here loves to donate to charities, especially at Christmas."

"James, you may leave now."

Kathryn shrunk away from the door, lingering just outside.

"What can we put your company down for?" asked Mr. Hardy, either missing or ignoring the cutting looks passing from George to James.

"I'm sorry, Mr. Hardy, James is entirely mistaken. I do not contribute to charities either during the holidays or any other time of year."

"But, surely," Mr. Hardy began, "you'll want to help your neighbors and community."

"No." The word was said with no room for argument. "Please leave."

Mr. Hardy's smile disappeared. He looked around the room as though looking for help from James to convince George to change his mind. With no help forthcoming, he turned his rotund person around and headed toward the door. Kathryn held the door for him and brought it closed, but he heard her softly offering a meager donation before the door completely shut.

"Shame, really." James said with as much disdain as George had ever heard.

"What?"

"You have so much and give so little."

"I work hard for what I have."

"But do you enjoy it?"

"What do you mean?"

"Do you enjoy your riches?"

"I think you're being ridiculous. If I gave it all away, I wouldn't be rich, would I?"

The glimmer of light that was always in James' eyes seemed to dim and George felt a twinge in his heart, but chose to ignore it.

James said goodbye with a repeat of his Christmas day invitation and left to return to his own job. The sweet wish of Merry Christmas he extended to Kathryn as he departed gave George pause, but again, he pushed the feeling aside and returned to work.

As George made his way home that night he found his thoughts pulled toward his interaction with James and the unrelenting smile on Kathryn's beautiful face. His sister, Adele had been like Kathryn, always sunny and good-hearted. James was so much like her it was almost painful. He missed Adele. If it hadn't been for her he wasn't sure how he would have lived through the years after their parents were killed in that car accident. Their grandparents tried, but granddad was so stiff and rigid. If it hadn't been for his sister and grandma he would never have known any softness in his life.

By the time he entered high school, Adele had left home and been married for two years. James' arrival was welcomed, but far too hard on her frail body. She didn't last three months after his birth. James' father, John, did a good job raising James and George was grateful his grandma wasn't burdened with yet another child. When his granddad passed away a few years later, George was glad he died before his grandma. But fate had it in for George and his grandma was taken to her rest not long after George graduated from college and long before he could boast to her of his business success.

Unlocking the door to the house from the garage he entered the kitchen, tossing his keys into the basket by the fridge. A cold breeze fluttered behind him and the hair on the back of his neck stood on end. A whiff of granddad's pipe tobacco teased his senses. Fully expecting to see granddad in the flesh, he turned and saw…nothing. The hum of the refrigerator sounded like a freight train running through the kitchen. George's palms began to sweat and his breathing became labored. Other noises intensified and although the normal creaks and groans of the generations-old house didn't usually bother him, at this moment they disturbed him greatly, and he quickly went through all the rooms of the big house to make sure everything remained as it should be.

Finding all well, he prepared a microwave meal of cardboard-tasting lasagna and sat down in front of the TV to watch the late news.

December broadcasts never changed. The news reported all the terrible things going on in the world and then at the end, related a story of some sap doing something nice for someone who was down on their luck. It happened every Christmas. George flicked off the TV and stood up. Restless and bored, he wandered into the room his grandparents had used as a library. The old books always seemed to provide some company, but tonight, one particular book pulled at him. He took it from its place on the shelf and rubbed his hand over the soft leather binding.

Granddad's journal. For some reason, the old, crotchety man had felt it necessary to write his life story, but he had been such an irritable, miserable person for so many years, George couldn't understand why anyone would be interested in reading about his life. He had never wanted to know what the old man said. It hadn't seemed important. Tonight, George felt a strange pull toward the book and he couldn't seem to put the volume down. He sat down in his favorite recliner and let the thin book rest in his lap. The feeling of someone watching him left him on edge and before he knew what he was doing, he opened the cover.

3

The early entries from his granddad's childhood didn't interest George at all. Unsure of what he was looking for, he thumbed through the pages until a date stood out. It was September 24th. A lump of lead fell and landed hard in George's stomach. The date was etched into his mind like an engraving in glass. And his heart was just as fragile. He remembered his reaction to the events of that night, but he had no idea what his grandfather had felt. He read the short entry.

September 24th. I am dead. I live and breathe, but my insides are dead. Today my son and daughter-in-law were hit by a drunk driver and killed. I am writing this down to relieve the awfulness I feel, but I'm uncertain as to its success. My heart is heavy and my mind feels like it's going to burst with tormented nightmares.

It wasn't too surprising. Everyone had been shocked that day. If it hadn't been for Grandma Ellie welcoming George and Adele into their home that night, George might have tried to follow his parents into oblivion. The entry that followed was written a few days later.

September 30th. Today I buried my son, Adam, and his wife, Anne. Their two children have come to live with us, but I have no enthusiasm for raising another child. Thankfully Adele is already a teenager, graduating this coming spring. George is young and lost and I do not know how to deal with him. I may send him away to school. It would probably be better for him and for us.

Well, George thought, it didn't take him long to decide to ship me off. George remembered being told he was going to boarding school. He knew he was supposed to be impressed, but instead he felt abandoned. Granddad had such a strong personality and had always been someone George looked up to. He couldn't have understood then that granddad felt inadequate. But he certainly understood how being away in school made their life easier.

A couple of entries were filled with business ideas and proposals he was considering. None of that mattered to George and he almost put the volume down when another date caught his eye.

November 28th. The Thanksgiving holiday was a shamble. What have we to be thankful for? Adam is gone. Anne is gone. Adele is preparing for college and spends most of her time at her friend's house. I should be glad, she seems to be handling her parents' death better than anyone else. George was very quiet when he came home for the holiday. He said he likes school, but it's difficult to get much more out of him. It's probably for the best.

George couldn't imagine how granddad could have expected anything else. Adele was so lucky. She was still living with them and could spend her time at a friend's house. George knew she was the easier sibling, but he never realized what a burden they considered him. The resentment he felt as a child flamed alive again and disgusted, he slammed the book closed and paced around the room. Still, in some ways, it explained certain things, like granddad never spending any time with George. A sadness seemed to vibrate off the now silent book and George couldn't seem to help himself as he picked it up again to see what it would say next.

Flipping back through the pages, the next entry was at Christmas time.

December 26th. Christmas is for wimps. I cannot abide the constant cheerful chatter I hear from everyone I meet. Do they not realize that some people are grieving? Eleanor says I'm becoming morose, but I can't help it. I am determined to spend my time working. Adam and Anne left nothing for their children. It all falls to me to provide for them. If nothing else, I can do that.

At this George felt somewhat of a kinship to his granddad. They both detested Christmas and all the superfluous cheerful goings-on. Focusing on work was his granddad's example and George had grasped that same principle for his life. There was nothing else for him. That focus pushed him to study hard and do well in school. But what George didn't understand was why he felt providing for the family was all he was worth. A shame, really, that they couldn't have talked it out. Perhaps it would have helped them both, but now it was all in the past. They could have used the time better instead of wasting it like they did.

George thought about his time in school and how the resentment continued to build that year. He didn't make friends and he didn't speak to anyone if he could avoid it. He studied all the time, working hard to do more and get higher grades than anyone else in his classes. His teachers were impressed, but his classmates steered clear of him. He had never felt so alone.

When George read his grandfather's entry in May, he understood a little more.

May 3rd. Adele came home today and announced that she is getting married. I was shocked. We haven't even met this boy she says she is in love with. Love. What a joke. The only thing love brings is sadness and heartache. Eleanor understands. But Adele is determined and after her birthday in two weeks, she will be of age and we cannot stop her.

George wanted to ask granddad questions about his entries. How could he have given up on love when he had a wonderful wife under his roof, in his bed? George had a hard time believing he had given up on so much because of his inability to work through his grief. Was that what George had done, too?

The grandfather clock in the hall chimed the late hour, long past the time when George usually went to bed. Getting to bed early made it easier to get up early and George spent his early mornings working from home before he went into the office at 7:30 am. But still, he couldn't put the book down. The thoughts and feelings his granddad had written reached into his soul to give him some kind of relief. Desperate for a level of comfort never before desired, he latched onto the words and searched for meaning in his life.

August 15th. It is almost a year since Adam's death. I cannot abide those who seem to think I can just let it go. I've tried for a year now to write how I feel and when I do, I just feel worse. At least I have my business. Eleanor understands.

The entries didn't seem to help, but George's granddad continued to write. There must have been some kind of therapeutic benefit. But his words denied its worth. Perhaps he didn't even realize good came from the writings. He kept saying Grandma Ellie understood, but his remembrance of her didn't jive with granddad's. He wondered where the difference laid. The next entry was several months later. George wondered if he gave up on writing because he didn't see the value. Intrigued with whatever imaginary push brought him back to the pages, he was surprised to see his own name.

January 5th. George returned to school today. He is such a quiet boy, I wouldn't mind if he was around more, but he says he would rather be at school. Eleanor is worried about him, but I assured her he will be fine. He's a good student and likes to study. He'll be a great businessman. I don't understand his love of all things computer, but I suppose it's the coming thing. He's probably better off without us.

That was the last Christmas he went to his grandparents' house. How did he miss his granddad's latent approval? He walked away that day and never knew things had begun to change.

Several of the following entries were all about his business, which had taken off while George worked his way through eighth grade geometry. He stopped at another date he recognized.

July 8th. Adele's baby was born today. The baby is healthy, but Adele has been so frail, we were afraid she wouldn't make it. The doctors feel certain she'll regain her strength. Her boy, James, cries a lot. George didn't come home this summer but went to stay with Adele. He'll be a help to them while Adele is getting better. I don't know what to say to George. He always has his head buried in his computer. His world is so different from mine.

George stopped reading to remember that summer. Adele had been so happy, so full of hope for a life of love and prosperity. John was a good husband and treated her like a China doll. He remembered her pale skin and delicate bones. But her excitement at the prospect of the birth of her child was intoxicating and he was caught up in her joy. Grandma Ellie wasn't happy when he told them he wasn't coming back there for the summer, but granddad told her he would be a big help to Adele. When the baby came and Adele was still so fragile, he did help. He learned how to make up a bottle, change diapers, and give James a bath. John worked during the day and George took care of the baby. When John came home at night, he took over the care of James and George was able to work on his computer. Why didn't granddad embrace new technology entering the workplace? His lack of living had never been so apparent.

Adele cooed and giggled after James was born. She rarely had enough strength to get out of bed, but she held James every afternoon and the love she felt for him, along with John and George gave George a sense of peace he couldn't remember ever feeling before that summer or since.

The next entry date stabbed George in the heart.

4

October 21st. God has forsaken us. If there is a God. Adele died in her sleep last night. She never was strong after James' birth and she finally succumbed to her frail body. Why does God punish us like this? What great sin have we committed that makes Him take away the people we care about? George left school and came home for the funeral. He packed up all his things and said he's not coming back ever. Eleanor thinks he'll change his mind, but I know he's in pain. He and Adele were very close. I don't know how to help him. But I'm sure he'll figure it out. I feel numb, as if all the liquid has left my body and I'm dry. I have no tears, nothing left.

George questioned God that day, too. He'd been in class when they called to tell him about Adele. He had collapsed in the headmaster's office. It was like reliving the day his parents died and he wanted to hurt someone or himself. They put him on suicide watch for days after he returned from the funeral. But he wasn't suicidal. He was angry. Every ounce of happiness he had known died with Adele that day.

George lifted his lips in a sneer when he read the Christmas entry. He knew granddad wouldn't miss him. He didn't even try to stop him.

December 24th. George called and said he's going away for the Christmas break. I can't imagine where he's going. He's not of age yet and I should demand he come home, but he said this isn't his home. I hadn't realized he felt that way, but I guess I understand. We've never been close. I'm sure he'll be okay.

And the funny thing was, he didn't go anywhere. He just stayed in the dorms, scrounged food from the custodian, and pretended he returned from Christmas break early when his other classmates started arriving. The confidence his granddad had in him sounded like the only way he could appease his conscience for never trying to have a relationship with George.

The next entry was marked four years later -

January 18th. George announced today he is opening his own software company with a friend from boarding school, Geoff McAllister. I'm glad to see him getting an early start in his business. It will put him so far ahead of the game down the road. He's grown up to be a fine young man. Eleanor says he's too serious, but I think he's on the right track. He doesn't come around, but he calls Eleanor regularly. Since he spends his summers with James and his dad, we've only seen him occasionally, but it's okay. I'm sure he's better off there than here.

George was surprised when there was a four-year lapse in journal entries. He assumed there wasn't much to say. George's high school years were more of a blur than he wanted to admit. If it hadn't been for Geoff McAllister, they might have been totally forgettable. When the two boys were assigned as roommates their senior year, they discovered a common interest in computers and many evenings were spent delving into the language of zeros and ones. George's final semester of high school was exciting as he and Geoff shared their dreams for the future and started putting together a business plan.

August 5th. George is going to college after all. He said he needs more education for running his software company. It's doing okay, but not growing as quickly as he wants. I encouraged him to continue his education. My own business is doing well and I spend a majority of my time there. Eleanor understands.

The reality of life after high school was a test of George's patience. He and Geoff weren't being taken seriously by the investors they met. No one wanted to do business with a high school graduate who had no intention of going to college. At the time, he didn't know which college would take him, but granddad's encouragement and financial support was the first time George remembered feeling any sort of connection to him. Granddad still talked about Grandma Ellie understanding him. As George registered the events of that first year in college, a twinge in his heart pricked at a memory he had stuffed into a back corner. But leave it to granddad to bring it up.

December 28th. George said he's met someone. It's Geoff McAllister's sister, Elaine. I wish George would just concentrate on his business and his schooling and forget about women, but I can't control that. At least he's determined to make something of himself before he gets married. He's too young anyway. He's smart and determined. He'll go far in his world. I'm sure he'll be just fine.

Elaine. Just the name made his heart bleed. He wanted to create what Adele had with John. He wanted a beautiful life with the same kind of joy and happiness. Youth and a lack of experience veered him away from the promise of happiness with Elaine. George had been swept away by her beauty and charm. He wanted to be everything she needed, but he was caught up in getting the software business going strong, strong enough to withstand any economic calamities. After a year of dating, he proposed and she accepted. But he kept putting off the wedding and Elaine got impatient. When Elaine broke off the engagement, George was devastated. He pretended he didn't care, but the truth was he was broken-hearted. She wouldn't wait until he could provide for her. He wanted to give her everything he didn't have as a child. He wanted their life together to be something special, but she wouldn't wait.

After Elaine left him, he shut down his emotions. Granddad had thought George would be fine, but he was far from fine. He had turned to his work and drove himself harder than ever.

Exhausted, George closed the book and set it down. He couldn't read any more tonight. The terrible ache in his heart zapped all his energy for the day. Certain he would feel better after a good night's sleep, he quickly got ready for bed, slipped between the sheets and fell into a restless slumber.

5

George wasn't sure he would be able to read any more of granddad's journal. Reliving his broken relationship with Elaine, he remembered that he had vowed he wouldn't let her leaving weaken him. What good would it do to go back to that time and see the mistakes he had made? She had moved on years ago and he heard she had married a good guy and was now a mother to three children.

Going into the office at the usual time, he fixed his gaze on a miniature Christmas tree sitting in the corner of Kathryn's desk. He didn't approve of personal items on his employees' desks. She knew the rules. Why did she do that?

So many questions. After reading granddad's innermost thoughts last night, George had more questions now than ever.

Kathryn came in at the usual time and peeked into his office with her morning greeting.

"Kathryn," he said, "I noticed the Christmas tree on your desk this morning."

The implication was there. He was sure he didn't need to elaborate.

The disappointment in Kathryn's arresting green eyes nearly convinced him to change his mind and let her keep the tree, but if he relented on that, where would it stop? He didn't approve of cluttered desks and if she did it, others would as well. He watched her until she couldn't look him in the eye any longer.

"I'm sorry, sir," she said sadly, "I'll put it away."

"Thank you."

"Yes, sir." The frown on her face clouded her eyes and, surprisingly, George found he missed her cheerful smile. But rules were rules. He got up and closed the door. It wasn't that Kathryn was humming this morning, it was just his habit.

Turning to his work for the day, he promptly forgot Kathryn's sadness and picked up the phone.

Kathryn wanted to throw something. Her normally sweet attitude turned sour. Mr. Stone was taking his usual unpleasantness down to new levels today. He looked troubled. Maybe there was something going on with the business that she wasn't aware of. Silently, she said a prayer that her job wasn't in jeopardy. She needed this job to help her family. Without her help, it would be so much worse for Elizabeth.

If Mr. Stone couldn't be cheered up with a Christmas tree, Kathryn thought, what would cheer him up? Then an awful thought crossed her mind. What if he didn't want to be cheerful? Did he want to be sad and bitter? What person would want such a thing? He was a walking puzzle for her. After working for him for three years, she still didn't know very much about him except that he worked all the time.

Every once in a while, when he didn't know she was watching, she would see him stare almost wistfully out the window. That softness she saw in his countenance called to her. She couldn't recall exactly when it had happened, but one day it was almost all she could do to stop herself from wrapping her arms around him and holding him close. Fortunately, she stopped herself in time to save her job. She knew if she attempted anything so forward and personal, she would be out the door without a second thought. Still, a part of her could see through the tough exterior and she was certain, deep down inside, there was a man in pain.

Determined to get somewhere with him, she decided to make cookies that night and bring him some on a plate. Surely, he wouldn't turn down a plate of holiday cookies!

George said goodnight as he left the office at 6:00 pm. Kathryn was staying late that night because she was going on vacation for the next few days. He still didn't know why he had approved the vacation time. Their year-end was coming up next week and they would be doubly busy starting in January. This month was the time to prepare for the extra work in January. Certainly, she had caught him in a moment of weakness, at a time when he couldn't foresee the impact of her being gone. Still, it was the first time she had asked for personal leave since she started with him. Technically, she earned the break. He just didn't understand what someone, who had a job, would do with time off.

With the image of her sparkling smile in his mind, he found himself once again in the den of his big, old house with yet another pasty microwave dinner on the tray in front of the TV.

The journal called to him. He pushed it aside, trying to focus on the news. The call grew louder. He actually got up, went into the library, and put the book back on the shelf. But before he could return to the den, the call turned into yelling. He turned, glared at the book and then felt stupid. What was in that book that he needed to read? So far, all it had done was make him feel horrible.

Giving up and feeling depressed, he grabbed the book and took it to the den. Switching off the TV, he slapped the book down on his tray, rattling the little plastic dish that had held his dinner. Stubbornly trying to put off the inevitable, he took the plastic dish into the kitchen and threw it away, cleaned up the few dishes in the sink and wiped up the counter. Finally, with nothing else to keep him from the den, he sighed deeply and made his way back to his chair and the ominous volume waiting there. Opening the book, he quickly found where he left off the night before.

June 10th. Today would have been Adele's eighth

anniversary. Her boy is growing up just like her, full of happiness, with a positive outlook. I think I envy him that. The doctors told me today my heart was giving out. I could have told them that years ago. My heart broke then and it's never been the same. But today they said it's more serious. I'm not sure if I care. Eleanor understands.

There! Proof that someone can just let themselves slowly die. Granddad never wanted to do much except work. It wasn't surprising his heart couldn't take the stress of running his business, never feeding his soul. He wasn't sure he agreed with granddad that Grandma Ellie understood. She understood a lot, but he made it sound like she agreed with him. George's phone calls to her became less frequent when all she talked about was his granddad's ill health and nasty disposition. George read on.

October 15th. Fall is a difficult time for me. Adam, Anne, and Adele. They're all gone and I have finally admitted that I miss them. Eleanor and I had a horrible fight. I thought she understood me all these years, but she said I was being selfish and now George is following in my footsteps and is just as selfish. His fiancée is waiting patiently, but I see an emptiness in him that my own emptiness recognizes. I wonder if I should have done something different. Eleanor threatened to leave me. I don't think I could survive her leaving. What to do.

So, the time came when even Grandma Ellie had had enough. It was too bad she didn't threaten him sooner. Maybe he would have lived longer or at least have enjoyed his life, however long it lasted. She thought George was selfish. That's what Elaine said, too, almost a year later when she calmly returned her engagement ring. But what was selfishness, but a concentration on one's life? He wanted Elaine to be a part of that, but he needed it to be when he was ready. Hearing that his granddad questioned his own actions was a little disconcerting. He had finally worked through his grief and it was too late. Would that be George's fate as well?

George looked ahead and saw there were only two entries left. A feeling of dread and wonder nearly overwhelmed him, as though he could see his past with a clarity he never had access to before.

May 24th. The doctors have given me only a few weeks to live. In all this time, worrying about my heart, they found something else to kill me. The tumors in my brain are inoperable and growing fast. I guess when you think you've got all the time in the world, you don't think about the long-term effect of the decisions you make. There's always time to make amends or change your mind. Now my time is gone and I've come to realize that my business will go on without me and my employees won't know the difference. They have never been important to me except for whether or not they did their job well. Eleanor cries all the time. I've let her down. She blames me that George never comes by anymore. I've been proud of what he has accomplished, but I guess I never told him. I hope Elaine softens his heart a little. She's good for him.

He knew he was dying. George had made a pretty good mess of things with his grandparents by then. Was he just a clone of his granddad, working his way into an early grave and never knowing the happiness that can come from life? Elaine didn't soften his heart before she gave up on him. How did he feel about his employees? Would they see a difference if he wasn't there? Suddenly his mind was filled with Kathryn's sweet, beautiful face and he knew if he wasn't there anymore, he would miss her. Would she miss him? Probably not. And that thought didn't settle well with him.

George drew another deep breath and turned to the last entry. What would it say? Would it make a difference?

July 6th. I know my time is short. I've been thinking over these last few weeks of all the times I've passed over the opportunity to be kind or forgiving or gentle toward my family. I've been so distraught from losing my son and my granddaughter that I've neglected those who were still with me. Eleanor barely speaks to me. George never calls or comes by. John brings James over regularly. They're the only ones who give me the time of day and even in their sorrow, their days are filled with the joy of life. Being around a dying old man isn't too fun and I understand. It's times like this when I wonder what life would have been like had I done things differently. Would George be here now, someone to talk to and keep me company in my last days? Would Eleanor and I be planning for a life after death? I'm not sure God is there anymore. But what if He is? What if He's been there all along and I've just ignored Him? How will I face a God I scorned and neglected in life? How I wish now I had a chance to start over. I don't want George to end up like me. I took Eleanor for granted and now she can hardly stand to be in the same room with me. I hope George will find happiness with Elaine and not allow his business to become his mistress. I tried calling him, but he won't take my calls. What can I do now? I guess I'll leave it in the hands of the One I've shunned and pray, yes, pray that George will somehow find answers before it's too late.

It was the longest entry his grandfather wrote. George was reeling from the revelation he spoke of. Did George believe in God? Had he really stopped taking his granddad's calls in those days? He knew he wasn't terribly kind toward James, but he never turned him away. Was that good enough? Somehow George didn't think so. Could he learn the lessons his granddad wanted him to learn before it was too late? He had lost Elaine. He *had* turned into his granddad! He knew he needed to change, but what should he do now?

6

When George walked into work the next day, he was surprised he missed the irritating humming of Christmas carols from the direction of Kathryn's desk that usually interrupted his morning. The quiet disturbed him. Convinced that his granddad's journal entries and their haunting quality carried the blame, he headed toward his office, intent to get through the several reports that were due to the auditor by the end of the year.

A cellophane wrapped plate of cookies greeted his eyes from the center of his desk. A grim line froze on his face as his eyes narrowed. He didn't like presents and he thought he had made it clear to his staff that he was immune to all things Christmas. A huffy sigh pushed from his lips and he picked up the festive tag that read 'to Mr. Stone from Santa.' Ha! He had no doubt the celebratory goodies were from Kathryn. She wouldn't have dared leave them for him except when she could escape the aftermath.

Without even peeking at the type of cheery sweets she had delivered, he hovered the plate over his waste basket, but couldn't bring himself to throw the treats away. Instead, he set the plate behind him on the credenza and turned on his computer. As he waited for the home page of Stone & McAllister to boot, the plate beckoned, calling his name like a whispering spirit. He found his eyes wandering to the shiny plastic wrapping and forced his gaze away from trying to determine what culinary goodies hid inside. It couldn't have been ten minutes before the plate urgently whispered again. Finally, with a frustrated grunt, he grabbed the plate and whisked the wrapping away, revealing over a dozen simple chocolate chip cookies.

He didn't eat treats. Did she know that? He tried to think of a time when Kathryn would have been privy to that kind of information. Their relationship was strictly a professional, working relationship. Did they ever discuss something as unrelated as dessert preferences? Still, the chocolate chip cookies looked so innocent and innocuous. Surely a single cookie wouldn't hurt. It looked very tempting. Without his permission, he found his hand holding a cookie and bringing it to his mouth for a taste.

The splurge of delicious brown sugar, butter and soft, smooth chocolate blended together to bring his taste buds into a chorus of symphonic harmony. Could anything else taste as delicious as this simple, completely ordinary gift? George took another bite and a little piece of ice shook free of his heart.

After forcing himself to eat a reasonable and healthy lunch, which he skipped most days to continue working, he couldn't resist taking a bite of another cookie on the plate. His mouth tried to find new ways to cheer for the tantalizing sweetness of each bite. George was reluctant to admit the delectable goodness, but his mouth couldn't lie. He hadn't had cookies like this since...since...and the memory of himself as a child playing in his mother's kitchen while Adele stood on a chair helping her mix batch after batch of cookies for the holidays regaled him. He turned in his chair away from the decadent delights and forced his attention back to work. He didn't need reminders of everything he had lost. Granddad's journal had done a thorough job of that and he was still recovering from the effects of his late-night reading.

Late into the afternoon, George searched the files on his computer only to discover incomplete charts integral to the report he needed for the auditor. Kathryn had promised to have the chart filled in so the information was at his fingertips. Disappointed with her unusual incompetence, he frowned and glanced back at the cookies, surprised by how many were missing. Would she have left the cookies because she knew she hadn't finished her job before her vacation? It wasn't like her, but he had known other employees who took advantage of the Christmas holiday season to slack off.

She wasn't due back until after the first of the year, but he needed those numbers so he could finish his report. He could crunch the numbers himself or he could call her and demand she complete the work she promised to do even though she was on vacation. It wasn't a matter of it being Christmas, he assured himself while he picked up the phone to call, she had simply shirked her work before leaving for vacation. It didn't matter whether it was December 23rd or June 23rd. He needed those numbers and he wasn't about to do her job to get them. Maybe it was time to start thinking about her replacement.

The phone only rang once before he heard Kathryn's lyrical voice on the other end.

"Hello?"

"Ms. Gleason."

"Mr. Stone?" The lilting voice disappeared to be replaced with somberness.

"Yes."

"Um. Is there a problem?"

George didn't waste any time getting right to the point. "You didn't finish your work before you left."

"I didn't?"

"You didn't complete the spreadsheet I need for the auditor's report." he asked.

"Oh, I'm going to finish it up here at home and bring it in the day I come back. You said you didn't need it until the end of the year."

"I said, Ms. Gleason, I needed it before the end of the year."

"Oh."

"I'll be by to pick it up after work. Please have it ready."

"Oh…okay."

Her obvious discomfort was satisfying enough for the drive to her house to be worth it, George thought. This would be a good lesson for her.

"What's your address?"

"Oh, I'm not at my house for the holidays. I'm at my parents' place. Couldn't I email it to you?"

"I don't want an electronic copy of this information passed

through the Internet. It's far too confidential and hacking is at an all-time high in our business. I certainly wouldn't let it sit on something as easily accessed as an email."

"I see. Well, I'm still at my parents' house."

"And that address?"

Kathryn gave George the address and he cringed a little as he wrote it down. He would need to drive another hour in the cold winter night to get what he wanted, but since he had demanded she get it done and told her he would be by to pick it up, he couldn't back down now.

"I'll be there around 7:30. That's not too late, is it?"

"No, that will be just fine, sir."

"Fine. I'll see you then."

With the conversation over, George eyed the remaining cookies. They would make a nice snack on the way to Kathryn's parents' house.

7

Pulling his suit jacket a little tighter, George hurried to his late model Volvo, placing his briefcase and the cookies in the front seat. After everyone had gone for the day, he carefully wrapped up the cookies in the saran wrap they came in.

Working his way onto the interstate, he checked his GPS and began following the mechanical directions. Fighting his way through the holiday traffic until he made it to the outskirts of the city didn't improve his mood. By the time he was an hour beyond the worst of it, he had all but forgotten the cookies resting on the seat beside him. As he glanced at his right side-view mirror, the highway street light dashed onto the forlorn package. Absently he reached into the makeshift bundle and pulled out the first cookie he touched. Delicious.

Four turns off the freeway, a pass through a small village, and three miles over rough road finally brought George to the address on his phone. The tinny electronic voice exclaiming he had arrived at his destination couldn't be right. The vibrant illumination of twinkle lights that glowed in the snowy driveway almost turned George around before he made it to the front door. Everywhere he looked screamed Christmas and he wasn't sure he would last long enough to receive Kathryn's report and avoid becoming truly ill with Christmas spirit. He dashed through the fat flakes of snow which had increased in volume since he started his trip.

The carol-singing doorbell caused his eyes to roll and the jubilant child who answered the door automatically made his scowl fiercer. Undaunted, the child pulled him inside the house and promptly shut the door.

"It's too cold outside to leave the door open." The child sounded as though she was repeating something that had been said to her many times.

The warmth of the home seemed to envelop George as he stood in the entryway. Everywhere he looked were signs of the Christmas holiday. From the shimmering Christmas tree in front of the living room window to the greenery adorning the fireplace mantle to the mistletoe hanging from the entryway light fixture, the house simply reeked of Christmas joy. George shuddered.

The little girl who had so graciously opened the door and ushered him into the house disappeared down the hallway, singing a silly tune he didn't understand. George stood there, dripping on the entry rug, and waited for an adult to come forward.

While he waited, he surveyed the festive decorations and saw through them to the dilapidated furnishings. The sofa framed one wall of the small living room in all its faded glory, surrounded by mismatched, overstuffed chairs that had been covered with thin sheets, tucked into the cushions and tied on with what appeared to be holiday ribbon. Even the ceramic nativity scene with the scratches and scrapes of years of enjoyment couldn't conceal the well-worn wood coffee table with one leg bearing a bolt that would do Dr. Frankenstein proud. Still, the candles dancing on the mantle and the sparkling lights from the Christmas tree, magnified by the tinsel hanging from every branch, gave the room a luster that any other time of the year couldn't accomplish.

Peeking beyond the living room to the dining table just inside the kitchen, he noted the numerous plates of cookies much like the one he had found on his desk that morning. Somehow George couldn't reconcile the sadly lacking furnishings with the look of abundance brought on by the dozens of cookies that looked to be gifts for so many. He silently criticized the poor decisions of Kathryn's family, obviously sucked into the traditions of a holiday they could apparently ill afford.

After several minutes, dripping onto the floor, George wondered if anyone besides the sprite who had disappeared down the hall knew he was there.

He called out, "Hello!"

Nothing.

"Hello!" he called again.

"Hello?" came the uncertain answer.

"Is Kathryn Gleason here?"

"Mr. Stone?" The woman behind the voice turned the corner of the kitchen and George drew in a surprised breath. Kathryn was covered head to toe in flour, a red apron with the image of Mrs. Claus fashioned across the front covering a forest green sweatshirt and jeans. Her bare feet peeked out from the bottom of her pants. Soft brown hair, which was usually held back in a tight bun for work fell from a loose pony tail and tickled the sides of her face. The brilliance of her dark green eyes gave the impression she had selected her eye color just for the holidays, but the glitter he saw in them shook him to the core. His staid, low-key, albeit sweetly humming assistant caused him to shiver and another chunk of ice melted from his heart.

Then she smiled and it was as though the sun came out in the middle of the room.

George tried to swallow and felt as though his legs wouldn't hold him much longer. He looked around for somewhere to sit.

"Please come in!" Kathryn invited. "We're just finishing the last of the Christmas cookies."

"I see. Thank you." George followed Kathryn into the kitchen where the heat increased, this time from the open oven door. He stopped at a chair next to the dining table and Kathryn motioned he should sit. She went to the oven, picked up a cookie sheet with uncooked balls of cookie dough neatly placed in even rows and slid it carefully onto the rack, closing the door swiftly. Before she turned around, she punched some buttons on top of the stove.

"Sorry. You caught me in the middle of baking. I didn't realize it had gotten so late." Before she could move a pot on top of the stove, it bubbled over and her attention was spent turning down the burner and checking whatever concoction she had cooking inside.

George watched, nervously hoping she would quickly be able to give him the report he had come for so he could leave the chaos of

Christmas celebration behind. Yet, seeing Kathryn in this environment, so at ease, so calm amid the storm of activity, so perfectly beautiful in spite of her layers of flour, faded jeans, and bare feet captivated his spirit and thoughts of leaving dampened his mood.

Shrugging off such ridiculous thoughts, he waited while she attended to the demands of the kitchen, taking the time to indulge in the cacophony of scents swirling through the room. Cinnamon and sugar competed with peppermint and coconut. George breathed it all in.

"Can I get you something to drink while you wait?" Kathryn said as she wiped her sticky hands on her equally stained apron. George wasn't sure what started out on her hands really ended up on the apron.

"Uh, maybe a glass of water," he said hesitantly. With the heat of the kitchen and the remnants of her cookies in his otherwise dry mouth, he needed a drink of something. Water would do.

"Sure thing." Kathryn reached into a cupboard and took out what looked like a mason jar and filled it with tap water. "Ice?" she asked, as she turned on the kitchen faucet.

George was overly warm, but he didn't want her to touch anything he would eventually drink. "No, thanks."

"Right. It's so cold out there, isn't it?" Kathryn smiled again and brought George the glass of water. She moved with a special energy that radiated around her.

George mumbled his thanks and Kathryn excused herself to attend to the pot on the stove and check the inside of the oven. The scene of pure domesticity shouted he didn't belong here and he twisted in his chair uncomfortably.

"I'll get the report for you in just a minute. I can't leave the cookies just yet."

"No problem." George heard himself say.

Just as George allowed himself to take a drink of the water, the little sprite from the door ran into the room squealing.

"It's snowing! Real hard!" she cried. "Maybe we can make a snowman tomorrow. It's Christmas snow, so we can make a Frosty!"

George was confused and other than the fact that it was snowing, he had no idea what the girl was talking about.

"Maybe," Kathryn agreed. "But first, I need you to set the table for dinner. With the cookies done, we can finally eat. Oh, I'm so sorry, Mr. Stone," Kathryn said, losing just a little of her bounce, "this is my niece, Caroline."

Caroline, now properly introduced, turned her attention to George and smiled. "We already met," she laughed. "I let him in. Is he staying for dinner?"

George looked as though he couldn't get away fast enough, and choked, "Oh no, I'm just here to get a report from, uh, Ms. Gleason."

Caroline giggled. "Ms. Gleason? Don't you know her name?"

"Of course, I know her name. I'm her boss."

"Oooh," Caroline said, drawing her 'O' out to cover several seconds. "You're that Mr. Stone."

Kathryn took Caroline by her narrow shoulders and turned her out of the room. "On second thought, go see if Maggie needs help picking up her toys and tell Thomas we're going to eat in a few minutes."

Caroline flashed a quick smile at Kathryn as though she knew very well she was being purposefully removed from George's presence and ran into the nether regions of the house.

Kathryn's abashed smile was a little endearing. George wondered what she had said about her boss that little Caroline might have spilled. He knew what his employees thought of him. It bothered him a little that his reputation had preceded him with someone so young and impressionable.

"Can you give me just a minute to get everyone settled and then I'll get your report." It wasn't really a question and George nodded.

He stood up. "I'll just wait in the living room, shall I?"

"Oh, of course," Kathryn said and waved him into the room situated only yards away from the kitchen table.

8

Kathryn wasn't sure what to think. The cookies had taken too long to put together. Caroline had wanted to help and Kathryn couldn't say no. The soup didn't get started on time and she had nothing else planned, so dinner was two hours late. Then Maggie, the youngest, whined for help with her fairy house and that took another twenty minutes. When Thomas asked for help wrapping the present he had so carefully made for his mom, Kathryn couldn't resist helping with that, too. Everything simply took too much time and then, on top of everything else, she had stopped as soon as Mr. Stone had called and finished pulling the numbers for the report he now waited for in the living room.

If her Mom, Dad, and sister, Elizabeth, along with her brother-in-law, Justin, hadn't been stuck behind a long line of holiday traffic in the city, she wouldn't have been here, all alone, babysitting and trying to finish up all the Christmas baking. Of course, Mr. Stone was on time. She was certain nothing happened in his world that wouldn't make way for his schedule. She knew he didn't celebrate Christmas. He mentioned it enough throughout December. She didn't know why, though, and even if he didn't allow any decorations in the office, she more than made up for it in her own little apartment and more so in her parents' little house.

Years of collecting clearance sale Christmas decorations had amassed quite an assortment of holiday cheer and everyone loved the gilded sheen of the decorations that brought out the true spirit of Christmas in an otherwise depressed atmosphere. With the sparkling lights and smell of greenery to warm the heart, the sadness of her world was kept at bay, at least for a short time.

Kathryn checked on the cookies once more, stirred the soup and quickly ran into the back bedroom where the three children were now watching a Christmas movie on Kathryn's laptop computer that she had brought from work. She knew the report needed to be done by the start of the New Year, but she wanted a way for the kids to watch their shows and she planned to have the report ready the moment she returned to work. She never thought Mr. Stone would need the report today.

Seeing the children were still following Frosty on his trek through the streets of town, she rushed back into the kitchen just in time to take the cookies from the oven. Quickly turning off the heat, she slipped the tasty morsels onto a cooling rack and put the still hot cookie sheet across the sink to cool. Pulling bowls and spoons from their respective cupboards and drawers, she set the table like an old pro, stacking the already plated cookies on top of each other to make room for everyone at the table. She poured a little of the aromatic broth into a small bowl for Maggie so it could start cooling. Standing for a minute, she debated whether she should ask Mr. Stone to join them for the meager meal or not, but her proper upbringing chided her hesitation and she immediately set another place for him. It wasn't much, but they could certainly share.

Unhooking the apron and draping it on the counter, she washed her hands and smoothed down her shirt. Never before had Mr. Stone seen her in casual clothes. She knew she looked a wreck, but it couldn't be helped now. Tugging her wayward hair back into the ponytail, she took the day-old bread she picked up at the bakery that morning and set it next to the soup pot.

"Dinner everyone!" she called.

Minutes later, two sets of feet hurried into the kitchen. Maggie's almost silent feet lagged behind and stopped in front of George who still sat on the sofa. Kathryn peeked around the corner from the kitchen and held her breath. She never knew what would come out of Maggie's mouth.

"Who are you?" Maggie said pointedly.

George seemed perplexed. "I'm Mr. Stone, Kathryn's boss."

Maggie just stared, then burst out with, "Why are you here? Are you going to take Aunt Katie away?"

Kathryn started to nibble on her lip and went into the living room to get Maggie. "Sorry," Kathryn began, "Never mind her. She was interrogating the grocery store clerk this morning."

George's lips twitched as though they wanted to smile, but weren't sure exactly how to go about it. "That's fine."

"I've set a place for you at the table," Kathryn said. "Please, won't you join us?"

George was uncertain. He looked from the table, where the two older children were already seated and waiting and back to Kathryn who picked up the little one, and carried her to a chair holding a large book on the far side of the table. He saw the bowl and spoon waiting for his decision. His stomach growled. The mismatched dishes and silverware, the sweetly innocent faces of the children waiting patiently to be served their soup and the irresistible beauty obviously certain he would say no found him answering her summons, and he was seated at the table at about the same time he realized he had accepted her invitation.

Kathryn secured the toddler on the big book in the make-shift booster seat and scooped the vegetable beef soup which occasionally included a chunk of beef into the bowls for the children. George tentatively handed his bowl to Kathryn and paused to watch as she obviously worked a little harder to gather a few more pieces of meat for his portion. Then, with everyone else served, she scooped soup into her own bowl and sat down. No one reached for their spoon.

Kathryn and the children bowed their heads and Kathryn asked Thomas to say a blessing on the food. After the simple prayer, Kathryn stood up again and sliced the bread, handing everyone a piece to accompany their soup.

George took in the watery beef vegetable soup, with bits of carrots, peas, small chunks of beef, and potatoes playing hide-and-seek with his spoon. The humble meal pinged his heart, but the children didn't seem disturbed at all.

Throughout the meal the children prattled on about the funny snowman they were watching on the video in the bedroom and how much they hoped it would snow enough for them to make a Christmas snowman, too. Kathryn laughed along with them and George felt a niggling memory trying to invade his consciousness. What was it about this scene that played on his mind?

The bubbling light was back in Kathryn's jewel-like green eyes and George found himself relaxing as he listened to the children rambling on. He wasn't required to join in, but they included him in the conversation anyway. He snickered at the way Caroline teased Thomas and at Maggie's outbursts. And through it all, Kathryn sat in the midst of them, in her element it seemed, and he allowed himself to wonder what it would be like if she was more than an employee.

9

When dinner was over, Kathryn stood up to clear the table. Maggie jumped down from her seat and marched over to George. With a big smile and her hand outstretched, she pulled him from his seat and dragged him down the hall toward the room she shared with her brother and sister. George's hesitant look brought another smile to Kathryn's mouth and as he disappeared down the hall, she called to him.

"I'll just get that report for you while you're busy with Maggie."

An answering nod was all she received before Maggie pulled him into the bedroom. Kathryn quickly retrieved the report from her own room, secured in its file folder, and placed it on the coffee table in the living room. Sending her eyes heavenward and whispering a little prayer for God's grace on behalf of George for the impertinence of Maggie, she headed down the hall to George's rescue.

The sight she found upon reaching the doorway to the children's room was something to behold. Having Mr. Stone in her house gave her the chills. But, she never, ever thought she would see George Stone, stern businessman, sitting cross-legged on the floor of the children's bedroom focused intently in front of

Maggie's fairy house. She almost burst into laughter.

But the scene was far from humorous. Their faces were dead serious as Maggie regaled him with the history of her clothespin fairy and how she came to live in the cardboard box that Caroline and Maggie had decorated into a fairy house with crayons and markers.

Maggie shared the story of Fairy Abigail's arrival with enough drama to satisfy even Shakespeare himself. Mr. Stone seemed to be totally caught up in the story, his gaze never leaving Maggie's animated one. As Maggie told the story, George would nod here and there, letting her know he was right there with her in the throes of Fairy Abigail's dilemma of where to place the windows in her new house. Even when Maggie reverted into her own baby language that only Caroline and Elizabeth, Maggie's mother, could understand, George's attention never strayed.

Kathryn's heart was full to bursting with the love she had for her little niece and a silly fluttering stumbled its way through her stomach as she saw a glimpse of the softer side of George Stone she never doubted. As Maggie finished her story with the grand ending of Fairy Abigail deciding the new fairy house was finally worthy of her residence, Kathryn cleared her throat.

"Oh, Kathryn," George said as he clumsily regained his feet, "Maggie was just telling me the story about the fairy who lives in that, uh, house there."

Kathryn couldn't hide the glowing smile and admiration she felt for his indulgence. This was a George Stone she had secretly hoped was hiding inside the gruff exterior he showed the world, but certain he had never let anyone else see. "That's fine," she acknowledged. "Maggie," she said as she turned her attention reluctantly toward her niece, "It's time for bed. Please start getting ready and I'll be in to help you in a minute."

"What about Tommie and Caroline?"

"They'll be in right away, too. Hurry now, and get Fairy Abigail put away for the night."

"Aunt Katie?" Maggie asked as Kathryn and George turned to leave the room.

"Yes, honey?"

"Would it be okay if Mr. Stone tucked me in?"

Kathryn turned a concerned look toward her employer. Was he

ready for something so intimate as that? After all, he had only come to pick up the report and she had already practically forced him to stay for dinner and listen to Maggie's favorite story. She looked to George for the answer.

George's expression wasn't the revulsion she anticipated, but neither was it the interest or excitement she was sure Maggie felt deserving of putting her to bed. The graciousness of his answer brought a lump to her throat and her emotions threatened to overwhelm her.

"It would be an honor, Miss Maggie." George assured her. "How long do you need to be ready?"

Maggie smiled her biggest grin and promised she would hurry.

Kathryn took George's arm gently and pulled him back down the narrow hall. Her hand turned warm where she touched his arm and she simply couldn't control the rosy blush creeping over her cheeks. She only hoped he didn't notice.

When they entered the living room, Kathryn waved him onto the sofa again and picked up the folder with the report inside. "Maybe you'll want to review it while you wait," she suggested.

"Of course," he said, "Good idea."

Kathryn excused herself to corral the other two children into the bedroom so they could prepare for bed, too, staying to help Maggie on with her nightgown and to watch all three children brush their teeth. Standing at the bathroom door, she frequently stole a look at George, intently reading the report in the living room.

Before Kathryn knew what was going on, Caroline rushed down the hall and grabbed a plate of cookies, turned to George and presented it to him. Standing there in her snowflake covered flannel nightgown, she waited for him to finish reading and see her hands stretched out with her offering.

"Merry Christmas, Mr. Stone," Caroline said sweetly.

"Oh, uh, I, um, I already," George paused to look for help from Kathryn, knowing he had already received his Christmas cookie present on his desk this morning. "I, uh..."

Kathryn found herself smiling again at his discomfort. "It's okay," she reassured him so he would accept Caroline's gift. "The other plate was from Santa."

Caroline's eyes got wide. "You already got a present from Santa?" she asked as George took possession of the goodies.

Kathryn stepped forward and rushed to cover her blunder. "Santa dropped by a plate of cookies for Mr. Stone last night. You know, I think sometimes he takes care of the grown-ups before Christmas so he can concentrate on the children Christmas Eve. Don't you think so, Mr. Stone?"

Quick to follow Kathryn's lead, George said, "Absolutely. You know," he said to Caroline, "your aunt is pretty smart. I'd believe her if I were you."

Caroline looked up to Kathryn with unconditional adoration. "Thanks, Aunt Katie."

"Okay," Kathryn said, "off to bed now. Mr. Stone is tucking Maggie in, but you all have to be in bed before he comes in."

Without further prompting, Caroline ran down the hall calling everyone to get in their beds so Mr. Stone would come down and tuck them all in. Kathryn cringed at how Caroline had misinterpreted what she said.

George set the report back into the file folder and stood up. Preparing for the requested tucking in, he squared his shoulders and took in a breath. He stopped when he heard Kathryn's chuckle.

"You look like you're going to meet the president and you don't know what to say," she said with a smile.

"You never know," he countered. "She may end up the president one day. I'll admit I'm nervous."

The touch of Kathryn's hand on his arm, twice now in the space of only a few minutes, was turning his insides to mush and his legs to jelly. It was as though her hand pumped warmth into his whole body and he could feel himself swelling from what was turning into a soft caress. His heart cried out for more, but his brain came back in control and told him he was imagining things.

"We're ready!" came the sing-song call from the bedroom.

George looked into Kathryn's emerald eyes, "They're ready." Still he didn't move. The swirling green mixed with gold in her eyes held him mesmerized and it wasn't until Kathryn removed her hand from his arm and took his hand instead that he broke contact by looking at their clasped hands instead. It didn't help. He still couldn't get past them standing there in her living room, holding hands.

Kathryn gave him a gentle tug and he followed her down the hall. As they entered the room, George noted that Fairy Abigail was secured in her house and it held a place of honor on top of the dresser. Each child sat on their respective bed, feet swinging excitedly, waiting for their turn to be tucked in. Maggie took charge.

"Mr. Stone?"

"Yes, Maggie?"

"Are you going to tuck in Tommie and Caroline, too?"

"Of course," George scratched his head and looked over at Kathryn. He wasn't sure what was more difficult, the idea that he hadn't a clue how to tuck a child in for the night or looking at Kathryn and suddenly not being able to think of anything but what it could be like to tuck her in. Oh no! Don't even go there, the voice in his head screamed. He turned his attention back to the children and figured he'd just wing it.

Bending over each child in turn and pulling the threadbare blankets over their little bodies, George couldn't help but wonder how they stayed warm at night. The heat of the fire in the living room couldn't possibly make it down the hall and the room felt chilled already. Perhaps their flannel pajamas were enough. He hoped so.

Standing at the door, he watched as Kathryn knelt down in the middle of the small room and led them in prayer before she stood and turned out the light.

"Sleep well," she whispered. "Tomorrow is Christmas Eve and we'll have lots of fun!"

George didn't stay for the whispered excitement that the next day would bring. He really needed to be gone. Being here had clouded his mind and melted his heart and he wasn't sure what to do with his unexpected feelings for Kathryn.

"Thank you," she said from behind him. "I know this hasn't been what you planned for your evening. I hope the children haven't been too demanding."

"It's been fine." George sounded a little gruff, but how could he explain that it wasn't from being upset by the children, but from being upset with himself.

"Oh, and thank you for accepting Caroline's cookie plate."

George didn't know what to say so he just raised his eyebrows in question.

"You see," Kathryn hurried her explanation, "we've been teaching them how much better it is to give than to receive. They won't get much for Christmas and the joy of giving is a difficult lesson for children their ages. Caroline's thoughtfulness needed to be acknowledged so she could feel that joy. I really appreciate you following along." The earnest sincerity clutched at George's heart again. "That is what Christmas is really about, you know."

"What it's really about?" George wasn't sure he understood since he didn't really understand anything about Christmas.

"Well, yes," Kathryn explained. "Besides the celebration of the birth of Jesus Christ and the gift of God's only Son, it's about the joy of giving and receiving. But even though it's nice to receive, sometimes, it's even better to be the one giving. And," Kathryn paused as though she wasn't sure she should go on.

George waited.

A determined look stole across Kathryn's face as though she had come to a conclusion. "And they don't have much. So, they don't have much to give. But they don't get much either, so the lesson is still important."

"I see," George said. He needed to think about this side of Christmas. But right now, he really needed to go. The night was gone and it would be a long, dark drive home.

10

George bent down and picked up the file folder with the report resting inside. He turned back to Kathryn with a question on the tip of his tongue, but he wasn't sure what he would say. He stepped toward the door. His mind told him to leave. His heart told him something more was happening here and he should find out what it was all about.

Kathryn reached for the door knob and looked into his eyes with a combination of coolness and fire. The world shifted. The sweet blush on her cheeks as she sneaked a peek at the plastic mistletoe hanging from the light fixture assured him his attraction was mutual and his attention wouldn't be turned away.

But this was Ms. Gleason. His employee, his assistant. It would be unseemly to take advantage of the holiday for such a trifle. Right? George hadn't been so unsure of himself since his first day of boarding school. Kathryn blinked. He needed to leave. As tempting as she was, he couldn't do this. It wouldn't be fair to her or to him.

"Thank you for the report, Ms. Gleason. And thank you for dinner, too," he added. He had no idea what to say about the children so he said nothing.

Her smile nearly had him undone yet again. "You're welcome,

Mr. Stone. And thank you for your indulgence."

When Kathryn opened the door, the whip of snow that snapped through the doorway left them both shivering.

"Wow," Kathryn said, "I had no idea the weather had turned so nasty. Are you sure you'll be all right?"

George peered into the dark night, the wintry scene illuminated by the colorful twinkling lights and sugarcoating the severity of the storm. "I'll be fine," he said absentmindedly, thoroughly distracted by what he imagined would be his drive home.

"If you're sure," Kathryn said. "If not, you can certainly stay here with us."

"Thank you for the thought, but it'll be fine." George cringed. He was repeating himself and he didn't sound any more convinced now than a moment ago.

Turning up the collar of his inadequate suit coat, he pressed the file folder against his chest and bade Kathryn a quick good night. Pushing out into the snowy wind, he couldn't rush too much without slipping. He finally made it to his car. Once inside the cold, dark vehicle, George shivered again and checked his watch. How could it already be 9:15?

Starting the car, George sat there while it warmed up and considered the poor but cheerful scene. He wondered where the children's parents were. Were they alive? Did Kathryn take care of them all herself? No, he reasoned, he knew she lived in town. She said this was her parents' home and that she was visiting for Christmas. But did the children live here, too? Were her parents raising their grandchildren like Grandma Ellie raised him and Adele? He remembered never being happy after moving in with his grandparents. No matter how much Grandma Ellie tried, the gloom and serious atmosphere in their home squelched all attempts at humor or lightheartedness.

He couldn't imagine what life would have been like with Adele if their home had been a happier one. Still, he thought, Adele had been happy. But not so much until she got married right after high school. George had been shipped off to school, too young to understand Adele's need to be out of the house and find her true self in her happiness with John.

A fearful sadness engulfed him as his mind replayed her death.

He hadn't thought about her in a long time and now he had relived his short time with her frequently in only a few days. The blizzard roared around his car, startling him from his reverie. He needed to get home and back to normal.

George turned the windshield wipers on high and checked his back window. The rear window defogger was working its magic and he had confidence that once on the highway, the speed of the car would prevent any more snow build-up. Carefully backing up to turn the car around and point down the driveway, his headlights glared into the blowing snow. Inching ahead, little by little he gained the much-desired distance from the twinkling house of Christmas cheer.

A dark shadow on the right passenger side of the car caught the corner of his eye and he instinctively hit the brakes. The shadow disappeared, but the back end of the car swerved to the right. Over correcting as he steered the wheel to the right, the rear end gave a good imitation of a figure skater dancing back and forth across the driveway until the left rear wheel hit the edge of the pavement and careened the car to the right where the front tires lost their footing and slowly, silently slipped into a three-foot ditch. The crunching sound he heard echoed in his ears.

George closed his eyes, not believing his horrible luck. He hadn't even made it out of Kathryn's driveway. Listening to the tires uselessly spin mocked the whirling in his mind. Now he would have to return to Kathryn's door, if only to call for a tow truck. He wondered if he was paying some sort of penance for not celebrating Christmas and now he would be shrouded in red and green and every other color of decoration until he saw the white snow in Technicolor. Leaving the deceivingly harmless file folder sitting on the front passenger seat, he opened the driver's door and braced himself for the onslaught of the storm again.

Irrational anger snuck up, slapped George in the face and he uncharacteristically slammed the car door as he stepped away. Sure enough, in keeping with the way his day had entered into an alternate reality, the car shuddered and slipped even further into the ditch. Another crunch. He cringed.

A small part of George almost wanted to sit down in the driveway and give himself up to the elements. But whatever it was inside him that fought for reason won over and he headed back to the shimmering door behind which he would find that breathtaking brunette.

The knock on the door took a while to be answered and he almost laughed at the look on Kathryn's face when she opened the door, still wiping her wet hands on the kitchen dishrag.

"Hi," he said lamely.

"Hi, yourself," she replied.

"Can I come back in?"

"Oh, of course." Kathryn stepped out of the way and George came in only far enough for the door to close behind him.

There he stood again, dripping onto the entryway floor and the déjà vu image didn't escape him. Kathryn raised the proverbial eyebrow in question.

"I...my car...I...it's in the ditch on the side of the driveway."

"Oh."

"I thought I saw something and I stopped too quickly. The car fishtailed and slipped into the ditch." Why he felt compelled to explain the accident to Kathryn, George didn't stop to examine. Something inside him didn't want her to think he was an irresponsible driver.

"It's pretty nasty out there. Please come in." Kathryn ushered him into the living room again. "Can I take your suit coat? It's really wet."

George shrugged out of the coat and Kathryn opened the closet door to hang it up.

"Excuse me while I finish up the dishes," Kathryn said as she headed for the kitchen with her dishtowel.

"Sure," George said, "I'm just going to call a tow truck. I should be out of here soon." He silently crossed his fingers it wasn't wishful thinking that gave him that idea. With the way his luck was going, he would be stuck in Christmas Tinsel Town for the rest of his life.

Pulling his phone from his pocket, he dialed information and frowned when he discovered he had no cell phone reception. Before he could put the phone back in his pocket, Kathryn returned with a phone book and a cordless phone.

"Good luck," she offered and then returned to the kitchen. "The first thing to go out here during a storm is cell phone service."

Did he hear a little chuckle in her voice? George grimaced. All his luck had been bad so far. Why would it change now? After locating a towing service in the local village, he called and spoke with the man who answered.

"Hello," George began, "this is George Stone. I need a tow truck to come to …"

"Slow down fella," the man on the other end of the phone said. "I'm sure you think I've got all kinds of trucks just waiting for every call, but it's just not like that."

"What do you mean?" George asked.

"I have one truck, Mr. Stone. It's already out on a call and I have three more calls waiting. I won't be able to get to you until morning. And that's as long as I can get anywhere in the morning. There's a blizzard out there."

"Yes, I know there's a blizzard."

"Are you in a safe place?"

"What?"

"Are you in a safe place? Are you warm and dry?"

"Oh, yes, I'm with my assistant at her parents' house. I can't remember the street name. Just a minute." George held the phone away from his ear as he called to Kathryn to ask her the name of her parents' street. George returned the phone to his ear.

"…and as long as you're safe, others are going to take priority. Why don't you call in the morning and I'll see what we can do?"

"You mean even though I called first, someone else will get serviced because I'm in a house with heat?"

"That's what I said."

"Are you kidding me?"

"It's about keeping people safe, sir."

George paused. "Fine, I'll call in the morning."

"Thank you, sir, Merry Christmas."

George hung up on the holiday wish and tossed the phone onto the sofa. "Oh, wait," George said to himself as he reached for the phone. He thumbed through the phone book again and mumbled a soft expletive when he didn't find what he was looking for.

"Problem?" Kathryn asked.

"Oh!" George jumped back. This entire situation had totally discombobulated him.

"Sorry." Kathryn moved into the room from the kitchen. Her

crossed arms floated down to her side and she sat down on the chair nearest to the Christmas tree.

"Yes, there's a problem. I can't get a tow truck and they won't even keep my spot because I'm safe and warm."

"I told you that you could stay here." She smiled and he swallowed hard.

"I know, but I thought I could at least go to a hotel nearby. I can't find one in the phone book."

"That's because there isn't one around here."

"Not one?"

"No, not one." Kathryn's smiled faded just a little. "You really are welcome here."

George didn't want to seem so ungrateful, but this was not a good idea. Being so close to someone who could now throw him so off kilter couldn't be a good idea. Standing up and putting his hands out to the fire to warm up, he knew he needed to make this right.

The unbidden image of his Grandma Ellie's sweet face going over the right way and wrong way to talk to people surfaced in his memory and he turned to Kathryn.

"I didn't mean to sound ungrateful," he said. "I just don't want to be a bother."

"I know," Kathryn's smile returned full force. "And you're not a bother."

"Thank you." George put his hands in his pockets and accepted his fate.

11

The doorbell reverberated in the quiet glittery house. Kathryn looked up with a worry on her forehead that stirred George's spirit.

"Who could that be?" she muttered to herself as she walked over to the front door.

The two men standing in the doorway with their arms full of paper grocery bags seemed entirely out of place at 10:00 at night.

"Kathryn, Merry Christmas!" the older of the two gentlemen said.

"Well, Harold! And Charles! What in the world are you two doing out in this storm? Please, please come on in." Kathryn backed up, holding the door and making space for the two gentlemen in the entryway.

"We're only here for a minute," Harold said as he and Charles shook off the snow from their winter coats. We have these bags for your family and the storm sort of delayed us. You guys are so far out, we thought you could use what's inside but, to be honest, we didn't want to take a chance that we couldn't get out here tomorrow." Harold held the bag in his hands out to Kathryn.

Taking the bag and setting it on the floor, Kathryn peeked inside and exclaimed over the contents. "Oh, mom and dad will be thrilled. This is so great! Oh, thank you, thank you so much."

Curious over Kathryn's exclamation, George got up to see what the commotion was about.

"Who's this, Kathryn?" Harold asked with a gleam in his eye.

"Oh, Harold and Charles, this is George Stone, my boss. He came out to pick up some work and got stuck in the snow."

George held out his hand to Harold and then Charles, "Nice to meet you, gentlemen."

"Your boss, Kathryn?" Charles said, doubt edging his voice. "I think he's more than just your boss. Here you are, on the eve of Christmas Eve, late at night, cozy in the living room..." he stopped, letting everyone else fill in the blanks.

George cleared his throat, "Oh, no, I'm just her boss. It's true. I was here to pick up a report and then I stayed for dinner and then Maggie asked me to tuck her into bed and I couldn't get out of the driveway and ended up in the ditch."

The oh-my-gosh-what-have-you-said look on Kathryn's face enhanced the sparkle in her green eyes as she tried not to laugh at George's ramblings. If they didn't already want to think of George as her boyfriend, his denial sounded so fake and him admitting to tucking Maggie into bed would ensure they wouldn't believe the truth now if she swore to it.

Turning the conversation back to the bags in an effort to distract the two men from George, Kathryn gushed, "This is just so nice of you guys. I know mom and dad can really use the food and the kids will be thrilled with the presents on Christmas morning."

"It's our pleasure. After all, it's what Christmas is all about." Harold and Charles exchanged a pleased look.

"So, George, old man," Harold looked him straight in the eye. "Do you want some help with your car in the morning? We can't help tonight, but we could be back in the morning and pull you out."

"Oh, no, I couldn't ask that of you," George was still stumbling. "I have a tow truck coming in the morning, so I'll be fine. I'm not sure I'll even be able to drive the car. There may be too much damage."

Kathryn gasped slightly. "Thank you so much for your offer Harold. We'll get it all figured out in the morning. Mom and Dad will be home soon and Justin and Elizabeth are with them, so we'll have lots of help in the morning."

"Well," Charles said, "if you're sure."

"Oh, I'm sure," Kathryn said in her sweetest voice.

"Well, young man," Harold said with a slap to George's back, "You take care of our sweet Kathryn, you hear? She's as wonderful as she is beautiful."

George swallowed hard, not because he didn't agree with Harold, but because his budding feelings were still so new to him and he certainly wasn't going to do anything about them. He attempted a glance at Kathryn, only to see the humor still dancing in her eyes. Apparently, she wasn't repulsed by the idea. It gave him pause.

"We've got a plow on the front of the truck," Charles said. "We'll go over the driveway before we leave. That way your dad doesn't need to worry about the snow until morning."

"Thank you so much!" Kathryn hugged them both.

Harold and Charles wished them Merry Christmas three more times before they actually left to brave the storm once more. George was glad they had what appeared to be a strong truck with a plow attached to the front bumper.

When George sat back down on the sofa, Kathryn joined him. He could feel her resisting the impulse to laugh. Her shoulders shook. She turned her head away, but she couldn't keep it in. George watched dumbfounded as she burst out with giggles. He was amazed by her. The more she laughed, the more a smile nudged the sides of his mouth. When she braved a look back at him, her giggles increased until he was afraid she would turn hysterical.

Her laughter was contagious. The noise that jumped from his own mouth surprised him. His laugh sounded foreign even to himself and Kathryn's eyes widened and she sobered a little, but wiped the joyful tears from her eyes while she grabbed onto George's arm for support. He couldn't remember the last time he had laughed. The lightening of his heart gave his mouth the freedom to lift and he smiled. The heat of Kathryn's hand seeped into George's spirit and he desperately wanted to reach for her, but a noise at the door froze his hand.

Kathryn's face went pale, all laughter ebbed, and she stood up and walked to the fireplace before the door opened. George wondered if he had only imagined the passing moment of hilarity.

The jubilant voices that entered the house silenced George's thoughts and he, too, stood up, but headed for the Christmas tree and as far away from Kathryn as the little room would allow.

"Kathryn! What a time we've had getting home. You wouldn't believe the traffic and then, oh my gosh, the weather!" Mary Gleason, Kathryn's mother, shook off her coat and absently reached inside the coat closet for a hanger. Her gray curls were covered in snow and she ran her fingers through her hair to shake the crystals loose.

"We were about an hour from town when the blizzard really hit," Henry Gleason, Kathryn's father, continued. "Almost white-out conditions all the way home. We saw drifts out there already three feet high and the radio said it's supposed to snow all night. We worried we wouldn't make it all the way home."

George shrank back further into the room, wishing he could just disappear.

"Mom, Dad," Kathryn tossed a glance at George. "We have company."

Mary's hand stopped midway to the closet rod. "Company? Tonight?" Her hand finished its journey into the closet and mindlessly closed the door. She didn't see Henry's wide-eyed smile as he reopened the door to hang up his own coat.

"Who?" Mary asked, as she smoothed her sweater over her dark slacks.

Kathryn motioned to George. He reluctantly stepped forward to be introduced.

"This is George Stone, my boss."

George watched the interaction between mother and daughter once Kathryn announced him. It was quite obvious his name had been mentioned before, but whether it had been taken in vain or not, he couldn't be sure.

"George Stone?" Mary held out his last name like she had never heard of him.

"Yes, Momma," Kathryn recovered first. "George Stone."

Mary turned to George and pasted a smile on her face that was as fake as Kathryn's was real. "It's so nice to meet you, Mr. Stone. To what do we owe this honor?"

"Please, call me George," George said, with an apologetic glance at Kathryn. After all, he hadn't even asked her to call him by his first name.

"Oh, thank you, George. Please call me Mary."

"Mary," George acknowledged and held out his hand.

Mary shook his hand and then referred to her husband. "This is my husband, Henry, Kathryn's father."

"Henry," George held out his hand again, "George Stone.

"George," Henry repeated. "You're here to see Kathryn?" The incredulity in his question almost made George laugh again, now certain whatever they knew didn't rate him high on anyone's list.

"I came out to pick up some work, but ran into some trouble with my car." George wisely left out the dinner and little Maggie's bedside invitation.

He could almost feel Kathryn's relieved sigh that he hadn't run off at the mouth like he did with Harold and Charles. Worried that Mary and Henry would get the wrong idea, just as Harold and Charles had, he looked away from Kathryn immediately, but not before he saw an uncertain look pass between her parents.

The kick at the door startled everyone and Kathryn practically leapt from the room to open it. George was beginning to wonder how many others would be coming over this stormy night.

"So, who's car in sitting in the ditch out there?" said a young man, similar in build to George. He filled the doorway, carrying a petite young woman in his arms, both of them smiling at each other in a way that, without words, told a story of true love. An instantaneous burst of jealousy clutched George's throat. What should he do with that feeling?

"It's mine," George said quietly.

"Hi!" the young man said, "Make way, folks!" The group parted and he swept the bundle in his arms into the house and deposited her on the chair closest to the fireplace, bending down for a swift kiss before he ran back out the front door.

The pretty young woman who had been carefully placed in the chair looked up at George, still with a dreamy look on her face. "Who's this, Kate?"

"This is George Stone, Ellie," Kathryn said slowly. "He's staying with us for the night."

The air chilled and George shivered as Elizabeth Black's expression turned to bewilderment. She narrowed her eyes at George. "Your boss?"

George wondered now if there was a doll in the backyard where they burned his image in effigy. He swiftly moved to Elizabeth's chair to offer her his hand. "It's nice to meet you, Ellie?" The name rattled him.

"Elizabeth."

"Oh, thank you. Elizabeth." George's relieved sigh was audible. He wasn't sure he could call her Ellie, but at the moment, couldn't explain why to this group of virtual strangers. Well, strangers except Kathryn.

"Ellie is Kathryn's older sister." Mary supplied.

"And the wonderful man who just ran outside is my husband, Justin," Elizabeth added.

"And," Kathryn continued, "the three children in bed down the hall are theirs."

"I see," George said. The chorus of information settled in his quaking brain.

A rattle at the door threatened to loosen what screws George had left in his mind. His quiet world at home seemed like a distant memory and he'd only been here for a couple hours. Henry opened the door and Justin burst in again, this time carrying a wheelchair.

"Oh, thanks, baby," Elizabeth said.

George watched in wonder as Justin set up the chair beside her and easily lifted her into it, stopping to tuck in a soft, but threadbare, blanket. Elizabeth pulled him down for another kiss and then said, "Justin, this is Kathryn's boss, George Stone."

In unison, everyone turned to look at George.

12

Justin offered George his hand, which George shook automatically. "Nice to meet you."

"I, uh, had car trouble," George stammered. "Oh, I already said that, didn't I?"

A round of nods waved through the room.

"Kathryn was gracious enough to invite me to stay," he plowed on, "the tow truck driver wouldn't come out since I'm not out in the weather."

Mary and Henry sent a silent message back and forth with their eyes and Mary turned, with her hands extended, "Of course, you're welcome to stay George. It's terrible out there. The radio said they're getting ready to close the roads to the freeway."

George swallowed. Not since he was a young boy had his world slipped so far from his control. And now he was trapped in Christmas house with Kathryn and her family? He looked at Kathryn and caught her soft smiling gaze. "You're very kind," he mumbled. "Thank you."

"Well!" Henry said as he clapped his hands together and George jumped. "It's late. Let's get everyone settled in for the night."

Kathryn tugged on her mother's sleeve and they leaned into

each other while Kathryn whispered in Mary's ear. Mary smiled and let her eyes rest on George briefly. Nodding to her daughter, she once again addressed George.

"We don't have lots of room, George. You understand. We already have a full house."

"Oh, Mary, I quite understand," George jumped in. He couldn't let Kathryn's parents be put out. It just didn't seem right. "I'll just take a piece of the floor here and I'll be fine."

"Don't be silly," Mary laughed. "I only meant to say that we don't have, you know, guest rooms and such, so we're going to give you the little bedroom in back of the kitchen. It isn't a fancy hotel like what you're probably used to, but it should do."

"I'm not used to a fancy hotel, Mary. I'm sure it will be just fine. Thank you, again."

"Of course." Mary nodded to Kathryn. "Katie, show George where he can sleep tonight."

"Yes, momma." Turning now to George, she said, "Mr. Stone?"

George could feel his face redden. At least this he could fix now. He followed Kathryn through the kitchen. She stopped briefly to touch the forgotten bags on the table. "Oh, momma," she called over her shoulder, "Harold and Charles brought over a couple of bags of goodies for Christmas. Oh!"

George almost ran her over, catching himself at the last minute with his hands on her shoulders. She looked up into his eyes and George could swear she swayed in his hands. "Oh, sorry, Mr. Stone."

"Kathryn," George sighed, his senses threatening to be overwhelmed by her sweet flowery perfume. Or was it her shampoo? "Please call me George. It's silly that everyone else in your family does and you don't."

"I didn't think you wanted me to," Kathryn said, her husky voice mocking George's rapid heart and seared hands as he continued holding Kathryn's narrow shoulders.

"I do."

The two words hung in the air for at least an age, until Kathryn coughed and stepped back. Another chink of ice slipped from George's heart as he took in Kathryn's wide-eyed expression and he silently thanked the universe that she appeared as rattled as he felt. At least he wasn't alone in this.

Kathryn stopped at the doorway at the back of the kitchen and George didn't have a choice but to squeeze next to her to see into what Mary had referred to as a bedroom. The single thing that could possibly make that true was the twin bed stuffed against the far wall. But the only way to move in the room resorted to squeezing along one side of the bed.

He peeked over Kathryn's shoulder and tried to focus on what she was saying. The tingle of her perfume tickled his nose again and it was all he could do not to bury his face in her hair. Willing his emotions to go back to the basement where they had lived the past fifteen years and his mind to shut up, he caught the last of Kathryn's apology for the undesirable accommodations.

"…it's not much," she continued, "but it will be quiet, away from the kids."

"It's more than I deserve," George muttered.

"Excuse me?"

Kathryn's question broke George from the overwhelming sensations he tried so hard to control. "I mean," he answered hastily, "it'll be fine."

Kathryn scooted into the room, completely filling the small space and reached for a handle protruding from the wall by the head of the bed. Reaching into the hidden cupboard, Kathryn drew out a pair of red pajamas and grabbed a bathrobe from the end of the tiny bed. Realization slapped George in the face and his heart dropped when he understood Kathryn was giving up her room—as though this could be called a room—for him.

"Wait," he said and Kathryn froze.

"I can't sleep in here."

"I know it's cramped," Kathryn began, "but…"

"No, it's not that." George took the silky pajamas from Kathryn's hands and placed them carefully on the bed. Surprised they both even fit on this side of the doorway, he took her hands in his and said, "This is your room, isn't it?"

Kathryn slowly nodded.

"I can't rob you of your own bed. It isn't right. I'll sleep on the sofa."

Kathryn's eyes popped and her face showed all kinds of worry. "Oh no!" she cried, "You can't sleep on the couch. If my parents found out, they would be upset with me. Be glad they didn't insist you take their room."

"What?"

"It's true. There is no way my parents would let you sleep on the sofa. I will."

"But that's not fair to you."

"But, George," Kathryn said, her voice calming, the soft tones wrapping around George's heart as it lurched to hear her say his given name, "this isn't about being fair. It's about giving the best you have to give for someone who needs it."

"I don't understand."

"I don't know how to explain it better. Just, please, let my parents offer you whatever they can. It will make them happy."

"Well, I don't know." George didn't get it at all. He ran his hand through his hair. "How will that make them happy?"

"Let's just say they don't have the opportunity to be host and hostess very often and this will please them. Think of it as a Christmas blessing."

George was confused. This whole evening seemed surreal. "Christmas blessing," he repeated. "I still don't understand, but I'll go along for your sake."

Kathryn smiled her thanks.

"Will you be okay?"

"Of course," she said, patting his arm and sending those pesky little shivers through his body again. "I've slept there many times."

13

Kathryn awkwardly squeezed past George to leave the room. The electricity between them was almost palpable and he would have bet money she felt it as much as he did. The buzz while she passed him emphasized the emptiness he felt at Kathryn's departure and added to his emotional strain.

It wasn't until he started undressing that he realized how out of place his shirt and slacks from work appeared. The elegant cut of his business wear shouted 'stranger' in the make-shift bedroom of the back pantry of an old farmhouse. And until this very moment, George would have agreed and embraced the 'stranger' label. Now he wasn't so sure he liked it for himself.

Loosening his tie, he slid it off his neck and rested it on the end of the bed. Pulling his shirt tail out of his pants, he unbuttoned a few buttons and then unhooked the waistband of his slacks. He looked around for a hanger, but the cupboard in the wall held only shelves and he couldn't see anywhere to hang his pants and shirt.

"Oh!" Kathryn's voice surprised George and he grabbed the wall to keep from falling over while his heart jumped around in his throat.

"I'm so sorry. I should have knocked. I didn't know you would get ready so fast," she said. The merry twinkling in her eyes as she looked him up and down in his disheveled state brought back that crimson rush.

"Did you want something?" George asked in his most boss-like manner.

Kathryn swallowed and her eyes burned into his. He hung his hands to his side, feeling exposed, even though he was still completely dressed. Had he said that wrong?

Kathryn recovered before George could answer himself. "I brought you these," she said, holding out a pair of plaid pajama pants. "They belong to my brother-in-law so they should fit. I thought you might be more comfortable in case you had to get up in the night…or something."

George couldn't stop the smile as he watched Kathryn's embarrassed face match his own for color. "Oh, uh, thank you."

Kathryn turned away quickly, letting him know how to find the bathroom as she hustled through the kitchen.

Two hours later, George laid on his back, his arms crossed behind his head and stared at the ceiling. Visions of Kathryn sitting at the dinner table, tucking her nieces and nephew into bed, and bringing him pajamas refused to fade away and let him sleep. The memory of her uncontrollable laughter echoed in his heart. Rolling over, he buried his face into the pillow and groaned. The scent of her soft floral perfume infiltrated his defenses until he gave in and relaxed. It was only then that he finally succumbed to a fitful sleep.

Walking away from George with his shirt tail loose, Kathryn stifled a giggle. It shouldn't be such a big deal, but no one at work would ever believe she had seen George Stone in such a state of undress. The skip in her step and lightness of heart shattered to the ground as she turned the corner into the living room.

Tears ran down Mary's face while Henry consoled her with an arm around her shoulder. Kathryn stopped short. The somber faces of Ellie and Justin, sitting next to the Christmas tree mocked the festive decorations and twinkling lights.

Kathryn sank onto the sofa and pulled up her legs so her chin rested on her knees. "So, what did the doctors say?" she asked.

Justin looked away and busied himself stoking the fireplace with another log. Mary and Henry looked at each other with a sadness Kathryn could almost touch. Ellie cleared her throat.

"It isn't hopeless," she began. "They can do the operation. We just can't afford it."

"What about the insurance?" Kathryn asked.

Justin stood and rested a hand on Ellie's shoulder and squeezed. The slight caress filled Kathryn with a longing she didn't recognize. "The insurance company said no. It's too experimental of a procedure."

"But others have been done," Kathryn argued, "and they were successful."

Justin's eyes closed and opened slowly. "Not enough."

Mary joined in, "There must be some way to get the insurance company to agree."

Henry shook his head.

"It's not like talking to a real live person," Justin said. "It's like they're robots reading it from some manual when you talk to them."

Henry crossed his arms. "We'll sell the house and the property in back. It won't bring much, but it might be enough."

"But where will we live?" Mary asked.

"You can't do that, Dad," Ellie said. "I won't let you. This place is all you have."

"I agree with Ellie, Henry, I can't ask that from my in-laws. Somehow we'll figure it out."

Ellie straightened her shoulders, letting Justin's hand slip away. "And if we don't, we'll just deal with it."

"But..." Mary interjected, tears filling her eyes again.

"No, Mom," Ellie declared. "This is my life. I'll play the hand I've been dealt. Let's not talk about it anymore. I won't get any worse before Christmas and I don't want our sadness and worry to affect the kids' holiday. It might be my last." Ellie's voice broke and Kathryn's heart ripped apart.

"Ellie," Kathryn's voice wobbled. "I have some money saved. I could give up my apartment in town and sell my car and give you everything I earn...and..."

"And how would you get to work, Kate?" Ellie's voice grew stronger. "You're going to give up everything for me and you think I'm going to feel good about that?"

Tears threatened behind Kathryn's eyes. "I want to help," she said, the meekness in her voice slipping it into a fog.

Justin squeezed Ellie's shoulder again. "Katie," he said, "relax. We're all a little edgy tonight. It wasn't the news we wanted to hear and we're all grasping at straws now to figure out a way to make it happen."

Ellie sighed. "I'm sorry, sis. I know you mean well. But you can't give up everything. I wouldn't let you anyway."

Mary turned into Henry's arms. A sniffle reached Kathryn's ears.

"Let's all go to bed," suggested Henry, his hands rubbing up and down Mary's back. "We'll face it again tomorrow. Who knows, maybe the insurance company will change their mind. Let's all pray for a Christmas miracle."

Everyone nodded and Justin flipped the lock off on Ellie's chair so he could roll her down the hallway.

Mary and Henry followed them, arm in arm.

Kathryn checked the front door and turned out the outside lights. Once she was ready for bed, she wrapped herself up in her blanket and stared at the Christmas tree for a long time.

14

Bacon! A wave of nostalgia crashed through George's dreams and he found himself in the midst of his sister's kitchen as she prepared breakfast. Her happy chatter matched the rosy glow on her cheeks. George laughed at the way she kept patting her baby bump.

"We have to come up with another name for you," she said. "Something more fun than Uncle George. It makes you sound like you're a hundred years old."

George laughed with Adele. "Sure, but it must be something dignified," George said.

"Like Uncle Boppy?" Adele offered.

"Just remember, Adele, you'll get a nickname, too, when the time comes."

George listened as Adele's laughter faded away and reality came crashing down.

The time didn't come. It would never come. Not for Adele. And George became Uncle George, not some fun-loving nickname for James to enjoy. When Adele died, all fun disappeared for George.

Opening his eyes and shaking off the dream, the scent of cooking bacon enveloped the tiny room where he had finally fallen asleep despite the heavenly scent of Kathryn's pillow.

Sitting up, a weight on the end of his bed kept his feet in place. There, on top of his neatly folded suit clothes, sat a stack of worn jeans and what appeared to be a flannel shirt. A pair of warm looking socks stuffed together in a roll crowned the pile of clothes.

George slipped out from under the covers without dislodging the pile. A slip of paper stuck out from under the socks.

George,
We figured you could use a clean change of clothes. Justin seems about your size, so try these on and let us know if they fit or not. Don't argue. Look outside when you can.
-Kathryn

George opened his mouth and then closed it tight. How did she know he would argue? And what was meant by the cryptic message at the end? Shuffling into the unaccustomed denim, George pulled the belt from his slacks and slipped it through the belt loops on the jeans. They actually fit pretty well. Surprised, he inspected the red plaid flannel shirt and snickered at what his grandfather would have said to see him in such casual clothes. Granddad's idea of casual was no tie. He buttoned the shirt and took a moment to enjoy the soft fuzzy fabric against his skin while he tucked it into the waistband of the jeans. Pulling the socks on quickly, he acknowledged his growling stomach and headed for the smell of bacon.

Conversation at the table stopped like someone had turned a switch when George came around from the back of the kitchen.

George didn't remember there being that many chairs at the table when they had dinner last night, but everyone was seated, including Elizabeth in her wheelchair. With the abrupt end to the discussion came the staring of all eyes on him. He stopped and self-consciously ran his hand through his hair. He probably had a bad case of bed head. He tried to unobtrusively check for anything left embarrassingly undone on his borrowed clothing.

As he opened his mouth to greet Kathryn's family, Maggie jumped down from her chair and rushed up to him.

"Mr. Stone!" Maggie grabbed George's legs and nearly knocked him over. He reached down and unclasped her arms, then knelt in front of her.

"How about a proper good morning hug?"

Maggie beamed. She threw her arms around George's neck and he answered her embrace. "Mr. Stone sounds a little too formal for a good morning hug. I think you should call me George."

Without letting go of George's neck, Maggie looked back over her shoulder at the hushed crowd at the table. Elizabeth's face puckered. George felt like a heel. His welcome last night must have been in his imagination. "Or not," he said.

Elizabeth's eyes met George head on. "It's just that we want the children to respect the adults in their life and calling you by your first name isn't as respectful as we would like."

"Oh, that's okay," George regrouped. He was a stranger and an unexpected guest. What should he expect?

"How about Uncle George?" offered Justin.

"Oh...that's not...nec—" George back-tracked.

"That's a great idea," Elizabeth said with a wink at her husband.

Justin smiled.

"Really?" Maggie's excitement was charged with an energy George couldn't pinpoint. "That's so great!" Turning back to George she squeezed his neck again and muttered into his shoulder, "Uncle George."

George couldn't decipher the stunned look in Kathryn's eyes and hoped he wasn't overstepping his place. But the way Maggie said Uncle George pierced his heart and he choked back a sob. How could one little person bring out his emotions so easily?

"I, uh, smelled the bacon," he said, hoping to distract from the little girl's affectionate display. "Is there any left?"

Kathryn stood, nearly tipping over her chair. "Of course. Please come sit here."

George paused. "I don't want to kick you out of your seat."

"Nonsense," Mary chimed in. "Katie was getting up to cook more bacon and some eggs. Come sit, George."

From Mary, it sounded more like a gentle command and he instinctively knew better than to argue. When Kathryn passed him on her way to the stove, he whispered a quick, "Good morning."

"I want to sit by Uncle George." Maggie wiggled out of George's embrace and raced back to the table, pushing at Caroline from beside the chair Kathryn had vacated.

"Hey!" Caroline protested.

"Mom!" they both shouted together.

Elizabeth threw an exasperated glance George's direction and then asked Caroline to please move over one chair.

"Caroline, please," Ellie said.

Caroline grunted as she reluctantly moved and Maggie climbed into the chair she left.

"I need my booster book!" Maggie said.

"Uncle George," Caroline said, ignoring her mother's hesitant look, "that means you have to be on my team when we play outside today, okay?"

George squirmed in the seat he took next to Maggie and searched Kathryn's face for direction.

The glint in her eyes as she glanced at him from the front of the stove told him he was on his own.

"Okay, Caroline, I'll be on your team. What game are we playing?"

"It's a race to see who can build the biggest snowman the fastest."

"Snowman?"

Caroline leaned her elbows on the table and rested her chin in her hands. "You do know how to build a snowman, don't you?"

Certain he would lose considerable points if he admitted to not knowing a thing about building a snowman, he nodded. He must have done it when he was little. "Of course," he lied. "Doesn't everyone?"

Caroline smiled and George figured he had dodged a pretty big bullet.

We're having bacon and eggs for breakfast," Maggie announced.

"That sounds wonderful," George said.

"It's a whole lot better than oatmeal," groused Thomas.

"Thomas." Justin shook his head.

"What? I hate oatmeal. We have it every day."

"Thomas." Elizabeth interjected this time and she looked uncomfortable.

"Well, we do," Thomas muttered.

Kathryn put a plate of hot bacon on the table. "Oatmeal is healthy and quick to make when breakfast is in a hurry, Thomas."

Elizabeth made sure the plate of bacon started with George and he automatically took three pieces. As the eyes of the children widened with each piece he placed on his plate, he suddenly felt guilty and picked up a piece from his plate and returned it.

"What are you doing?" Thomas asked incredulously.

"I think I took too much," George explained, watching the table of adults, watching him. "I'm not used to eating with a big family."

"Your family is small, George?" Mary asked.

George passed the plate back to Elizabeth. How to answer that? He shifted in his seat. "I, uh, don't live with any of my family. I only have one nephew and he's married."

"What about your parents?" Mary tenderly urged.

"Mom," Kathryn interjected. "I told you, George's parents passed away when he was young and his grandparents are gone, too."

"Yes," George didn't like the way the conversation centered around his lack of family, but he couldn't let Kathryn take the brunt of her family's inquisitiveness. "And my sister died several years ago as well. My brother-in-law took a job about two hundred miles down state, so I really only have James, my nephew, and his wife close by."

This discussion needed a new subject. George was about to mention the weather when Maggie affectionately stroked George's arm and said, "We understand, Uncle George, our mom's dying, too."

The heavy silence was thick with sadness and George felt as though it was entirely his fault for bringing the otherwise lively group into a speechless stupor. He sneaked a piece of his bacon over to Maggie's plate and was rewarded with a big grin.

The tension eased and Henry asked Justin a question about his work. The children concentrated on their bacon and Kathryn returned to the table with a plate of fried eggs.

"One or two?" Kathryn asked.

"Oh," George hesitated, looking around the table where, once again, all eyes rested on him. "One. Thank you."

Kathryn's smile brightened the entire room and George grinned back before he could stop himself. What was it about this house that made him drop his guard?

By the time breakfast was over, George committed to spending time with each of the children at various times of the day, which worried him since he was planning on leaving right after breakfast. He didn't want to disappoint them, but he couldn't stay. Every moment in Kathryn's family's presence caused an odd sensation in the pit of his stomach and at the same time a lightening of his heart. Certainly not unpleasant, it still bothered him.

"Kathryn," Mary said, "Dad and I are going to deliver the plates of cookies to the neighbors this morning. George," Mary paused as the breakfast dishes were collected and taken to the kitchen sink, "be a dear and help Kathryn with the dishes. It is Christmas Eve, after all."

"Mom." Kathryn's protest was only half-hearted. "He's a guest."

"It's okay, I'd love to help Kathryn." George joined her by the sink with his dirty plate.

"You don't have to do this," Kathryn whispered fervently.

"I want to," he assured her. "At least I know how to wash dishes."

"You do?"

"Sure. I wash my own."

"Don't you have a housekeeper?"

"Of course not. I cook and clean my own house, too."

"You do?"

"I do."

Kathryn dropped the plate she was washing into the soapy water and splashed the counter with soapy bubbles. Her blush only enhanced her rosy complexion and George snickered.

15

With the last dish put away and the wet towels drying on the oven door handle, George and Kathryn wandered into the living room.

"So, I'm assuming you saw my note," Kathryn said.

"Yes. As you see, I'm wearing Justin's clothes." George moved his hands to his hips and took a pose, standing tall, like a proud lumberjack.

Kathryn worked at keeping her mouth in a normal smile as she attempted to stop herself from bursting out in laughter. "It's a good look for you."

"Really? I haven't worn jeans since I was a little kid. My grandfather didn't allow them in the house."

"It's a good look," Kathryn repeated. Of course, she thought, he would look good in anything. How could anyone grow up not wearing jeans? Kathryn thought she knew everything about George since she had been his assistant for three years, but she realized now there was so much more to his past that she didn't have a clue about.

"Take a look outside," she pointed to the living room window, partially blocked by the now unlit Christmas tree.

George walked over to the window and peered out at the blinding white winter wonderland outside. Slowly, he started identifying lumps of snow in the yard as trees and shrubs.

"Uh, Kathryn," George's eyes narrowed as he searched more closely, "where's my car?"

Henry came up beside George and slapped him on his back. "It's that big lump over there."

George followed Henry's pointing finger and a little pinprick of panic seized him. "I was planning to leave this morning."

Henry chuckled. "I don't think so, George."

"But, sir, I can't stay here. I'm in the way. I need to go into the office."

Henry's chuckle deepened. "George, it's Christmas Eve and it's Saturday. No one works today. Looks like you're stuck with us."

"But..."

"Don't worry about it, son."

Henry's reassurance eased George's mind, but the term 'son' jarred him and pleased him at the same time.

"Tell you what, George, Mary and I discussed it and we'd like you to stay for Christmas. You can participate in all our holiday activities and then Christmas afternoon, after dinner, Justin and I will dig you out. Sound fair?

"Oh, more than fair, sir...I couldn't possibly."

"What's all this 'sir' nonsense? The name's Henry."

"Henry."

"Then it's all settled. Justin said he's got another change of clothes you can borrow and Mary found a new toothbrush in the pantry. You're set, son."

"But Henry," George couldn't seem to let it go. "I know you don't really want me here."

"George. You are more than welcome in our home. We have a pretty simple policy around here. You're welcome here whenever you like, but we expect you to accept us however you find us."

"I still don't want to intrude Henry."

"Well, then, we'll leave it up to Kathryn, shall we?"

Kathryn's head popped up and she shot a dart at her father. "I would love George to stay."

"How can I refuse?" George gave up.

"But the deal still stands," Henry teased.

"The deal?"

"You have to participate in all the holiday festivities."

"Oh," George considered. "I think that sounds like a fair trade."

Kathryn smiled.

"If," George continued, "Kathryn agrees to accompany me."

Henry grunted and muttered, "As if you could keep her away."

"Mom," Kathryn pleaded with her mother later as they made the children's beds together, "Dad practically forced George to stay. How could he do that?"

"Now, Katie, why are you objecting? Don't you want him to stay?"

"Yes, of course," Kathryn whispered before she thought twice. Grimacing, she continued, "But only if he wants to stay."

"Sweetie," Mary said as she patted Kathryn's hand, "I think he does and he's just polite enough to argue. It's endearing."

"It's not endearing."

"Now, you don't worry your pretty little head about it. I heard the children talking about going outside to build those snowmen. You should make sure George has a warm coat and some boots. Your father and I are heading out to deliver those cookies in a few minutes."

"Yes, ma'am," Kathryn agreed. Her half smile betrayed her true feelings. Feelings she wasn't ready to admit out loud to her mother and certainly not to George.

Kathryn headed for the porch behind the kitchen to search for some appropriate outer wear for George.

"Uncle George!" Maggie and Caroline sang together, finding him in the living room, playing a game with Thomas.

"It's time to go outside." Maggie rushed toward George and flung herself into his arms. He stood and swung her around before depositing her on the floor. Caroline's green-eyed frosty look tugged at Kathryn's heart as she watched from the kitchen. She could sympathize. Then she berated herself for lumping herself in the same category as Caroline and Maggie.

If she was honest, she wanted a whole lot more than a swing in his arms. The memory of their spellbound gazes the evening before brought the butterflies in her stomach to life. "Jingle Bell Rock" twisted and shouted and she mentally told the butterflies to sing "O Little Town of Bethlehem" instead. They weren't listening.

Uncrossing her arms and making her way toward George from the doorway, she shooed Maggie and Caroline away, explaining she needed to find George a coat and boots so they could go outside.

"Kathryn."

George's mild demeanor surprised Kathryn and she turned to listen. "Yes?"

"Thank you."

"For what?"

"For letting me stay."

"You didn't really have a choice, you know."

"Sure, I did. But I'm glad I'm staying. I really like your family."

Kathryn warmed to his words. "I'm glad you're staying, too," she whispered.

George smiled.

"Uh, let's find you a coat and boots."

"I can hardly wait."

George stopped to catch his breath. He had no idea building a snowman would be such an active sport. Caroline became a staunch foreman as he followed orders and rolled a ball of snow around the yard. She wouldn't let him stop until it was obvious he couldn't move the ball any farther. Proclaiming that spot as the perfect place for the snowman to stand, she immediately demanded they start on the middle ball.

George shook his head at Caroline's unrelenting directions and looked longingly across the yard at Kathryn and her crew of Maggie and Thomas while they struggled with their own ball of snow. Kathryn stood and their eyes met for a moment. George wasn't sure what had made the difference since he arrived, was it only last night? Yet the pull of attraction yanked him like a yo-yo and he no longer wanted to resist.

A slap of cold, icy snow hit George's chest. Giggles penetrated his frozen ears.

"I think we've just been assaulted, Caroline." George let go of the snowman body and picked up a handful of nice, wet white stuff and started packing it into a nice, wet white ball.

"Snowball fight!" yelled Caroline.

Another ball of icy crystals careened past George's shoulder, missing its mark this time. George took aim and sent his high and slow toward its target.

Kathryn screamed as she watched the long, high lob, completely missing the missile attack at shoulder level. Three hit their mark and Kathryn was drenched in soft powder. Maggie and Thomas burst into hysterical laughter.

George moved closer, another snowball ready, and Kathryn backed up, turning for the back fence and running as fast as her heavy boots and the knee-high snow would allow.

George's longer legs followed more rapidly and Kathryn screamed again as he came within arm's length and teased her with a snowball, still poised in his hand.

"You wouldn't dare."

"You started it," George's eyes twinkled.

Had she ever seen George's eyes sparkle like that? Maybe when he'd been angry. But he wasn't angry now and Kathryn pulled in a deep breath as she found herself drawn into George's deep brown eyes and matched their intensity.

Time slowed. "Oh!" Kathryn's foot slipped and she fell back, landing softly in the cold blanket of white. George relinquished his snowball, followed her into the snow, and held himself above her while he shook cold, white crystals from his knit hat over her face.

"Stop! Please. You win." Kathryn laughed. "I give!"

"What do you give, Kathryn? What do I win?"

George asked so seriously, Kathryn had to look carefully to make sure he was still teasing.

"What do you want, George?" Flirting wasn't really her style, but he brought out the tease in her.

George's eyes flitted over her face, stopping at her eyes and then moving on to her mouth. Her lips parted of their own accord and George leaned in.

"Oomph!" George grunted when three little bodies all jumped on him and pushed him against Kathryn. "I'm sorry. Are you hurt?" he asked in her ear, barely above a whisper.

"I'm great," she answered, the eyes glimmering back at him with unfulfilled promises.

George licked his lips and pushed the kids off his back. Kathryn was fairly certain she heard him say, "Later," before he turned and pretended to attack his assailants.

16

An hour later, two magnificent snowmen proudly stood guard in the backyard, sporting stick arms, rock mouths, and tattered old hats on top of their misshapen heads.

Standing in front of the dining room window with mugs of hot chocolate, courtesy of their sweet benefactors last night, Kathryn and George admired their morning's work.

"You were great with the kids, George," Kathryn said discreetly.

"They're great kids," George's voice sailed through Kathryn's spirit and she wanted to pinch herself to see if this was all real. "I don't think I can remember a time when I had so much fun in the snow."

"Oh, George." Kathryn leaned into his tall frame.

"Tell me about your sister, Kathryn."

Kathryn sighed. Fragile as a bubble, her happiness popped and she turned a sad eye to George. "She's dying, just like Maggie said."

"Is there nothing that can be done?"

"Her case is rare, affecting her spine. The usual medicine hasn't helped and she gets weaker and weaker. There's a new surgery they want to try, but it's considered experimental and the insurance company won't cover it."

Kathryn didn't like the next part of this story. It wasn't that she was embarrassed for being poor, but she hadn't yet been convinced it was something to be proud of either.

"We can't afford the surgery without insurance helping. It's as simple as that."

"So, without the insurance?"

"She won't live to see another Christmas."

George tucked a stray section of hair behind Kathryn's ear and drew his finger down her cheek. She leaned slightly into his touch. She wanted him to kiss her in the worst way, but the subject of her sister wasn't exactly conducive to romance. And when did she start thinking of George romantically? Oh yeah, about two years ago.

"I'm sorry, Kathryn."

"Yeah, me too. It's why we're going all out this year, while Ellie can at least enjoy watching the kids have fun. Next year, well, we just don't know..." her voice faded and George's hands clenched into a fist.

"Yes," he said. "I know only too well."

"Oh, George," Kathryn reached up and caressed his cheek. "I'm so sorry. You really do know. I've been so insensitive."

George took her hand from his face and linked their fingers. "Kathryn, you are the most sensitive person I can imagine. You have nothing to apologize for."

Kathryn looked down at their hands woven together and George softly brushed his other hand over her hair.

"I'm going to lay down for a while. I'm afraid I didn't sleep all that well last night."

"Oh, George, I'm so sorry!"

George stopped her lips with his finger. "Shhh. Stop apologizing. It wasn't your fault. It wasn't the bed or the room or the house. There's lots of nights I can't sleep. Last night happened to be one of them."

Kathryn wanted to kiss the finger that still lingered on her lips, but a sudden shyness overcame her. She stepped back and George dropped his hand. "Okay," she said, "you get some rest. There's still more fun to come later."

"That's right," George agreed, a smile playing around his lips. "Later."

The memory of that word and their almost kiss in the snow warmed Kathryn's heart and she watched as George made his way back to her tiny bedroom.

"I'm not sure I can stand all this romantic tension, sis," Elizabeth said as she quietly rolled alongside Kathryn.

Kathryn clutched her chest. "Oh Ellie, you scared me."

"He's different than you described," she said as she raised her eyebrows. "Where's the ogre?"

Kathryn's sardonic smile couldn't be helped. "I'm in big trouble."

Ellie laughed, a sound Kathryn hadn't heard in forever from her sister. Kathryn smiled sheepishly. "I guess I've been pretty hard on him for a long time."

"Whenever you talked about him, it sounded like he deserved it. He was controlling, miserly, and grumpy."

"He always gave off such negative vibes, but underneath I didn't believe it. He never talked about his family, so I only knew what I could find out from work or casual comments dropped by his nephew, James, whenever he'd stop by." Kathryn followed Ellie into the kitchen where they took out a roll of summer sausage and brick of cheese, courtesy, again, of the goody bags from the night before. Kathryn grabbed a knife and began unwrapping the sausage. "I guess it's really been James's devotion that led me to believe a good man lives somewhere deep inside George."

"I gather you're seeing a different side of him here."

Kathryn laughed outright. "You could say that. He told me this afternoon that he'd never had that kind of fun in the snow before. Can you imagine? What must his childhood have been like?"

Ellie reached up from her wheelchair and squeezed Kathryn's hand. "Maybe he just needed a chance to see what else is out there. He lives alone, right? He probably doesn't see much of normal everyday life."

"You call our family normal?"

"Well, when it comes to love and family, yes. I know there are horrible things in the world. I know my situation isn't ideal…"

Kathryn sniffed and fought a tear that threatened.

"…I also know we are blessed beyond measure with how much

we care about each other, help each other, and all the other selfless acts you see here all the time. My children are learning how to cope with the bad things that happen to good people and they will be stronger for it. I've accepted God's plan for my life. Remember, death isn't the enemy."

Kathryn leaned down to give her sister a hug. "I know. I just can't imagine life without you."

"Well," Ellie said as she straightened the blanket covering her lap. "Let's not talk about it anymore 'till after the new year. I really want this holiday to be special, you know."

"I know." Kathryn paused. "If I don't say it often enough, Ellie, I want you to know how much I love you."

A tear drizzled down Ellie's cheek and Kathryn knew her strong front was just that, a front. "Take care of Justin and my kids when I'm gone, okay?"

Kathryn passed Ellie a towel from the stove. "I promise."

Ellie accepted the towel, wiped her eyes and passed it back to Kathryn so she could do the same. "So," Ellie drew herself up as much as she could while sitting down, "it looked like you two got a little cozy out there in the snow."

Not the subject change Kathryn was hoping for, but since Ellie already knew about her secret crush, she supposed there wasn't any point in hiding.

"I think he was going to kiss me."

"Whoa!" Ellie chuckled. "That's some progress for a couple of days. Is there something in the snow? Is it magic Christmas snow?" The teasing glint in Ellie's eyes made Kathryn laugh again.

"Sometimes he's hard to read, but I think the children, especially Maggie, brought out a side of him that was buried deep. Then, when he leaned toward me and I waited for the kiss, all the kids jumped on him!"

"The little turds."

"No, probably for the best."

"Well, there's nothing to stop you later, after they go to bed."

"Right," Kathryn agreed with a secret smile. "Later."

17

An hour later, George emerged from the back-pantry bedroom, as he had begun to think of it, feeling refreshed. The short sleep had done him good and he felt lighter, as though a clean, fresh breeze had swept through his whole body, removing all the cobwebs and dust. The lure of steaming hot chocolate slowed him to a stop in front of the range.

Kathryn was reaching into the back of the cabinet under the sink when George voiced his appreciation of the intoxicating aroma.

"Oh!" she exclaimed, clamoring to stand up and accidentally banging her head on the top of the cabinet opening. "You're awake."

George held her elbow until she was steady. His fingers sizzled. "Yes. Are you okay?"

"Sure," she said as she rubbed the top of her head. "I was just coming to wake you. Did you have a good nap?"

"I did, thanks."

Maggie appeared at the entrance to the kitchen, running full bore into George's legs. "I had a good nap, too, Uncle George," she said as she hugged his legs.

George bent down and lifted the little girl high over his head, a smile stretching across his face. "I'm so glad. What are we doing this afternoon, Maggie? More snowmen?"

Maggie looked over at Kathryn. "Auntie Katie?"

Kathryn chuckled. "The rest of the day is in town, honey. We're going to sing around the Christmas tree, have some snacks, and then go to the community center for a candlelight service."

"I get to sing and hold a candle?" Maggie's eyes lit up.

"Um, yes, as long as your mom and dad say it's okay, I guess."

George squatted down to Maggie's level. "If they say no, you can share mine, okay?"

The adoration on Maggie's face startled George. He felt his face heat and mind race to understand what to do with this emotion. His own unplanned response and the desire to do whatever he could to make sure Maggie enjoyed her time in town wiggled inside him for dominance. He looked at Kathryn for confirmation.

Kathryn's look of adoration nearly knocked him over and the heat on his face was joined by the rapid beating of his heart.

Without warning, the image of her laughing while he shook snow over her face overwhelmed him. He stood suddenly and held his hand out to Maggie. "Hey, Maggie girl," he said, looking back at Kathryn's knowing grin, "let's go find your mom, then I'll help Aunt Katie finish up the food preparation."

A couple hours later, Justin opened the door and stomped his snow-covered boots on the front porch. "The driveway's clear! Is everyone ready to go?" he called into the house. George had offered to help shovel the driveway, but Justin refused. With a softly spoken comment about the need to think while he worked on the mindless task, George backed off and gave the man his space. He knew only too well how important that time could be under the circumstances.

Loading everyone into Justin and Ellie's older Suburban made George feel like they were going away on a week-long trip instead of into town for a sing-along. Besides the coats, hats, mittens, and boots, they stowed away Ellie's wheelchair, Maggie's stroller, and a combination of snacks along with two thermoses of hot chocolate. With everyone finally bundled into the car, George was exhausted. Squeezing this close to a family of people he didn't know should have been uncomfortable, but having Kathryn nestled at his side in the backseat managed to drive those feelings away. He debated about trying to hold her hand, but with her father on the other side of her, he hesitated.

He had heard of something called sensory overload from a business associate who had gone skydiving for the first time. Something about certain senses turning off because too many were fighting for recognition and the brain couldn't handle them all at once. That's how he felt. Too many emotions, though. Too many thoughts. Too many memories. Yet every time his thoughts became too much for him to bear, one look at Kathryn's beautiful face and cheerful smile calmed the attack and he could breathe again.

"Justin, baby," Ellie asked her husband, "would you drop me at the little gift shop across from the Christmas tree? I need to pick up one more gift tonight."

"Are you sure?" Justin asked. "Why don't you tell me what you want and I'll get it for you."

Ellie laughed. "What if it's for you?"

"Oh." Justin glanced at his wife with a silly grin on his face and reached around Caroline, who was sitting in the middle of the front seat, to rub Ellie's shoulder. "Is it?"

"Why Justin Black!" her delighted voice admonished. "You bad boy! You're as bad as the kids."

"Aw, come on Ellie." George saw Justin's wink in the rear-view mirror. "I just wanted to help you, sweetheart."

Kathryn snickered.

"Nice try, baby." Ellie twisted toward the back of the car. "Kathryn, would you help me with the shopping I need to do?"

"Of course."

Memories flooded George of his sister Adele's home and her husband John before James was born. They'd had that same kind of easy-going, teasing relationship. At the time, George didn't realize it for what it really was—true love. He thought about James and his wife, Jenny. Did they have that same contented and relaxed bond?

Looking back through an adult's eyes at the only time in his life he saw something like it, he longed for a relationship of his own that carried that same brightness and light. He did?

George squirmed in his seat until his right arm was free to drape across Kathryn's shoulder. Kathryn leaned into him and the car grew roomier.

Henry glanced between George's face and his hand, resting on Kathryn's shoulder, with a bit of a question mark.

George forgot Henry sat so close. He started to take his arm back when Henry smiled and slightly shook his head. George relaxed and let his arm fall back where it belonged. Belonged?

The glittering holiday lights turned the white snow into a kaleidoscope of rainbow colors. Every store front displayed Christmas scenes from Santa Claus and his sleigh to nativities. Red and green banners adorned doors and windows, railings and fences. The enormous Christmas tree standing front and center in the little park, that marked the town square, captured George's attention. He had a hard time believing he'd driven through this village only yesterday and missed all the decorations.

Scads of holiday revelers roamed the streets and gathered in the park. George couldn't believe all these people lived nearby. Daylight waned. Dusk turned to evening. Soon it would be completely dark.

Justin parked in the handicapped parking in front of the decked-out gift shop Ellie indicated and everyone piled out, reversing the ordeal of bundling into the car. The sidewalks had been cleared of snow and salt spread to melt the lingering slush. Henry unloaded the wheelchair as Justin reached for Ellie. Once she was comfortable with her blanket wrapped tightly against the cold, Kathryn turned to George.

"We won't be long," she said, her eyes vacillating between his face and her family. "Go with Justin and save me a place, okay?"

Justin punched George lightly in the arm. "We'll take care of George, Katie," he said with a smirk. "You take care of Ellie. And call me," his voice taking a serious tone, "if you need any help."

Kathryn nodded and cast a lasting look over her shoulder as Justin herded the kids across the street. George watched until the women disappeared inside the store, then quickly caught up with Justin and the gang.

18

By the time Kathryn and Ellie joined their little group standing about middle of the crowd around the big Christmas tree, night had fully descended. The blaze of lights couldn't diminish the chance to see Kathryn make her way to their side.

Justin took over the wheelchair and Kathryn sidled up next to George, pushing close to his side and slipping her gloved hand into his.

George smiled, happy she had the same idea he had while waiting for her, but he wanted a little more. He let go of her hand.

Kathryn's face shot to his with a worried look.

"Hang on," he said. He quickly took off his glove, shoving it into the pocket on the other side of his coat. Then he raised Kathryn's hand, slipped off her mitten and stowed it in her pocket. With their hands now bare, he quickly linked them together and brought her hand with his into his empty coat pocket.

"That's so much nicer," she whispered.

George murmured his agreement.

"Santa Claus is Coming to Town" came to an end and the choir director began leading the group in a rousing rendition of "Jingle Bells."

"Well," George said, "at least this is a song I know."

"Everyone knows 'Jingle Bells!'" Kathryn laughed. "I think it's the most popular Christmas song anywhere."

"But," George said, embarrassed, "I don't know any of the others. At least, I don't remember the words, just the titles."

"Not to worry. I brought a cheat sheet."

"A what?"

"The perks of being your executive assistant." Kathryn pulled a small songbook from her far pocket and showed George the title. *Songs of Christmas*.

"You always think of everything, don't you?"

"I try."

"I haven't told you lately how good you are at your job, have I?"

Kathryn laughed. "Have you ever?"

"Ouch."

"Oh, George, I'm sorry. I don't know how I let hurtful things out of my mouth."

George squeezed Kathryn's hand nestled deep inside his pocket. "Nothing I don't deserve."

"But I shouldn't say it. I shouldn't even think it."

"Yet it's the truth. I'd rather have you tell me the truth than hide your feelings."

"Really?"

An awareness enveloped them and Kathryn's eyes locked with George's. He saw something he'd never seen in them before. Well, except maybe when he was going to kiss her in the snow. More than acceptance, deeper, more meaningful. Was it possible she was as attracted to him as he was to her?

They joined in the last verse of "Jingle Bells" and Kathryn readied the songbook for the next song.

Carol after carol, they stood and sang, holding hands, except when Kathryn needed two hands to find the words to the next song. Once the page had been found, she quickly returned her hand to his pocket and rested it in his warmth.

A cloud cover blocked the stars and the air warmed slightly, although Kathryn wondered if she even needed her coat when she was holding George's hand. His strong baritone, albeit sometimes off-key, joining with the others sent a surge of happiness so exquisite through her body, she almost cried.

A short announcement by the choir director spotlighted the people responsible for the sing-along and the crowd offered muffled applause through gloves and mittens. A light flurry began and choruses of 'oohs' and 'aahs' waved through the joyful carolers. "Silent Night" was announced as the last song, with an invitation for everyone to join together at the community center for the inter-denominational candlelight service about thirty minutes following the sing-along.

If snow held magic, Kathryn thought, Christmas snow should bring miracles. As she sang the gentle tune about a babe born of a virgin so long ago and the salvation of the world because of his birth, she prayed for a miracle for Ellie.

Crackers and cheese made their way around their little group after the singing and hot chocolate followed. Kathryn was amazed George didn't even hesitate sharing the thermos cup, although they gave one to the children and the adults shared the other one.

Kathryn was glad George took her hand again as they made their way to the community center, like they had crossed some invisible bridge and entered into a new phase of their relationship. But would this new phase last when they returned to the city? After all, Christmas was tomorrow and then George would be leaving. Would this, could this, continue? Would he turn back into the Grumpy Gus he was before he was trapped at her parents' house for Christmas?

Kathryn contemplated options and scenarios as they entered the multi-purpose room of the community center and found seats in the back. She didn't want to go back to cold shoulders and formal discussions. What could she do to preserve what they achieved in two short days? One day, actually.

"It really filled up fast, didn't it?" George asked, looking over her shoulders at the crowded room.

"It always does. It's a great tradition."

"Hmmm."

Programs and slender white candles, fitted with drip skirts were passed down the rows. Kathryn was forced to relinquish George's hand and missed the warmth immediately. George took his candle, stuffed his program in his pocket and wrapped his arm across Kathryn's shoulder. Even through her coat, she could feel the warmth return. Seemed he missed the contact, too. Kathryn couldn't stop smiling. Maybe keeping this thing going in the city wouldn't be so hard, after all.

Kathryn watched Maggie push her way down the row, stopping in front of George with big, sorrowful eyes.

"Uncle George," she whined sadly, her pouting mouth drooping in her biggest frown, "Mommy and Daddy said I can't hold my own candle. Will you still share yours with me?"

"It would be my privilege, honey," George said, hiding his reluctance to let go of Kathryn from all but Kathryn. He picked Maggie up and rested her on his hip, holding the candle in his unoccupied hand. Maggie's hand joined his and she grinned at Kathryn in triumph. Kathryn wondered about her instant flip of emotions, the little manipulator.

Kathryn shoulder bumped him. "Later," she promised.

She noticed George tried to stifle his smile.

19

The lights in the large hall dimmed and the crowd hushed. Even little Maggie settled into George's arms, while everyone waited for the program to start.

A processional of robed teenagers began walking from the back of the room, slowly making their way to the front where a stage and choir bleachers had been set up. Each robed youth carried a battery-operated candle and a reverent, peaceful feeling swirled around George.

The faces on the performers were calm and focused. A single light beamed down from the ceiling at the front of the podium. The choir started singing quietly "O Come All Ye Faithful," the hymn building with each verse until each choir member was standing in their place behind the minister. Father Pratt introduced himself and the other members of the ministry who were sponsors of the evening.

Never before had George witnessed a community so connected that even religious bounds were crossed. Father Pratt's message was subtle and concise, fixing on the birth of Jesus Christ and his purpose on earth. Reading from the second chapter in Luke, George recognized the words, but couldn't think where he had heard them before. He didn't remember his parents being particularly religious and couldn't recall seeing a bible anywhere in his grandparents' house. But the words swelled inside him and he listened carefully.

The choir sang again. This time, "O Little Town of Bethlehem."

Following the choir, Pastor Richardson introduced himself and spoke, as well, about the birth of Christ and his ministry on earth. Had George ever considered why Jesus came? Was it important? He hadn't given it much thought through the years. Yet his granddad's last entry in his journal still plagued George with the uncertainty of doubt.

Another choir number, this time the short hymn, "Hark the Herald, Angels Sing" and George could feel his heart lift from the words of the song. He noticed Kathryn's furtive glances and needed to switch hips as Maggie relaxed in his arms. She was fading away and getting heavier. But he was determined not to put her down. Somehow, her faith and optimism in his goodness made it impossible to fail.

Kathryn laid her hand inside his crooked arm and it felt to George like the world had righted itself. He stood taller and squeezed Kathryn's hand into his side to acknowledge her welcome presence.

When Pastor Richardson finished his remarks, children entered the room from the sides and took up their spots on the stage to set the scene for the nativity. Once again, the scriptures were quoted from Luke, Chapter 2, and Mary and Joseph made their way down the center aisle toward the stable. The choir sang "Away in a Manger."

As Mary and Joseph passed each row, an usher followed, lighting the candle of the patron on each end and indicating they should light the next candle in the row and so forth until all the candles were lit.

"Maggie," whispered George, "it's time to hold the candle."

"Hmmm?" Maggie's sleepy response stirred George's heart. What would it be like if this was his child?

"The candle," he said, "I need your help holding the candle."

"Oh. Yes. Thank you, Uncle George." Fully awake now, Maggie held herself firm, giving George's arms a chance to gain a little circulation and gently wrapped her tiny hand around his.

By the time Mary and Joseph took their places beside the tiny manger, baby Jesus appeared and all the candles were lit inside the silent room. No other lights remained and the effect was as though the candles were starlight from that first night when Jesus came to earth.

Father Pratt asked everyone to join the choir singing "Silent Night" and George was grateful they had sung it outside so the words were fresh in his mind.

Peace washed over him. Kathryn's hand held him steady and he breathed deep the power of the contentment that sank so far down into his soul.

When the song ended, a prayer was given and the candles were blown out. Once the ushers collected the candles, Maggie gave George a big hug and thanks for sharing his candle.

Such a little thing, thought George, but obviously quite important to her. He kept trying to find a word to describe his feelings and finally settled on the one that summed up his entire visit with the Gleasons—happy.

No one seemed in too much of a hurry to rush home and with the slow pace, George continued to carry Maggie back to the car while everyone else trailed along. Once Ellie was secured into the front seat and everyone else buckled up, Justin took them home. No one spoke and George assumed they were simply caught up in the moment of the program, reflecting on their own beliefs, hopes, and dreams.

Before they took off their outer clothes, Henry announced they were going to gather around the fire outside in the backyard for some more caroling to end the evening. Then the children were off to bed.

George couldn't believe the evening had come and gone so quickly. It saddened him that it would be over soon, that tomorrow he would be leaving for the cold, lonely house which awaited his return. It dulled his spirit a little to think of it.

Henry lit the fire he had prepared before they left for town and everyone warmed their hands as they stood around the fire pit, this time singing the bouncier tunes of Christmas. "Jingle Bells" managed to garner an encore and George laughed.

After all the singing, Henry asked everyone to bow their head and he led them in a soulful, stirring prayer that thanked God for all their blessings, their family gathered together, and surprisingly to George, for his attendance with them. He wasn't sure when was the last time someone was glad to have him around.

Justin bustled the children into the house after the prayer and Mary pushed Ellie inside. Henry made sure the fire was safe, throwing a heap of snow on top of the flames.

George took Kathryn's hand. "I don't know how to tell you how much this day has meant to me."

Kathryn's simmering emerald eyes showed her happiness. "I'm so glad. I have to admit I was nervous at first, but you seemed to have had a good time today."

George blinked rapidly, suddenly caught up in more foreign emotions. "The best time I've ever had, Kathryn."

Kathryn reached around George and gave him a hug. "Well, the night may be over for the kids, but it isn't for us."

"Oh?"

"Yes, the next tradition is to get into our PJs and meet in the living room to talk and drink hot chocolate…and such."

"That's the tradition, eh?" George teased.

"Yes, well, Ellie and I used to do it all the time, but I think we'll have the room to ourselves tonight."

"So," George nodded, "PJs in five minutes?"

"I'll meet you there."

George pulled open the outside door and Kathryn slipped down the hall.

20

George couldn't ever imagine being this casually dressed in front of Kathryn and her family, yet it all seemed so normal. Maggie's cries took his attention again.

"Please, I want Uncle George to do it."

The request couldn't be mistaken, but George wasn't sure what she wanted him to do.

Hushed voices he couldn't quite understand countered the crying child.

"But just ask him." Maggie pleaded loudly.

"Fine." Ellie didn't sound happy and George wondered if he had overstepped himself in their home. The feeling depressed him.

Kathryn exited the kid's bedroom and quickly approached George, standing just inside the living room.

Her smile eased his conscience a bit, but he still worried.

"Have I done something wrong, Kathryn?"

"Oh, no. Maggie just wants you to tuck her in instead of her mom."

"Oh, I couldn't do that to Elizabeth."

"No," Kathryn picked up his hand to pull him down the hall. "It's okay. Ellie's okay with it."

George reluctantly followed Kathryn.

The tension in the room nearly sent George back down the hall. He didn't know what to do. Would Elizabeth hate him for it? Would Maggie hate him if he said no? He chafed at not knowing.

Henry walked up behind him and placed a strong hand on his shoulder. "Go ahead, son, it's okay. She's sad Maggie has chosen you over her, but she wants what Maggie wants tonight."

"I don't have the right to be here, sir," George protested in a soft whisper, his throat thick with emotion.

"George, you're our guest. You have every right to be here."

Henry's rich timber buoyed George up and he caught Elizabeth's hesitant nod.

"I'll make you a deal, Maggie," said George.

Maggie looked up with red rimmed eyes and waited.

"I'll tuck you in, but your mom kisses you last and says the prayer, okay?"

"Okay," came the tiny voice.

"Me, too?" asked Tommy.

"And me?" asked Caroline.

George chuckled. "Yes, everyone."

The air grew easy and light and the children slipped into their beds. George made a major production of pulling the covers over each child and tucking them in tight, promising sweet dreams and Christmas magic.

Elizabeth smiled her gratitude for George's words, kissed each child, and then brought her wheelchair to the center of the room for the final prayer of the evening.

Peace once again restored, Kathryn watched from the doorway, bowed her head for Ellie's prayer and peeked at George as he quietly stood and closed his eyes.

What was he thinking, she wondered? The stern, driven businessman who entered her house a little over twenty-four hours before had vanished. The man she saw now, so casual, so easy, so pleasant gave her goosebumps and she sent up her own silent prayer that this George would stick around long enough for them discover something more than friendship. Her plans for the evening didn't come close to romantic, but she hoped George could feel the Christmas spirit and would be, perhaps, swayed a little by it in how he viewed the world. Only time would tell.

Scooting down the hall, she stepped into the kitchen to stir the hot chocolate, simmering on the stove. Pouring two mugs full, she deposited them on the coffee table in the living room and returned to the kitchen for a plate of cookies.

All was ready.

Mary winked at her from their bedroom doorway and she giggled.

Kathryn saw George shake Henry's hand and kiss Mary on the cheek. Such a show of affection dropped her jaw and she coughed to cover her surprise.

Could this be real?

Christmas Eve was full of magic and with courage normally suppressed, Kathryn boldly watched as George sauntered down the short hall, making eye contact with her and holding it until he stood so close she had to look up. A wave of cinnamon rushed past Kathryn and she drew in a deep breath, catching the scent of George the man and focusing on not wrapping her arms around him. Not yet.

The absurdity of the situation grabbed Kathryn by surprise and she felt the giggle erupt into full out laughter as they stood there, staring at each other. George's eyes widened and his brows raised in question. Kathryn reached for George's arm to keep from falling over as the hilarity of them standing in their pajamas in the middle of her parents' living room on Christmas Eve threatened to break her brain. Laughing until only a cough remained, George's concern for her shone from his face and he gently led her to the sofa, where he sat next to her and waited...patiently.

Kathryn fought for composure and finally won, taking in big gulps of air as her heart rate settled into what had become a normal racing pace whenever George was near. This wasn't what she had in mind for an intimate conversation in the living room. She didn't want to scare George away just as she felt she could possibly win his affection.

"There aren't many presents under the tree," George said.

And in a heartbeat, the laughter was gone and Kathryn was

sober. "Oh, George," Kathryn said as she took his hand in hers. "It isn't about the presents."

"But the children…"

"They've never expected much. It's fine."

"I don't understand."

"There's so much more to Christmas than presents, George."

"I'm beginning to see that. The singing and the program tonight was amazing. I've never heard or seen anything like it."

Kathryn reached over to the mugs of hot chocolate and placed one in George's hand. "Here, have some hot chocolate."

George chuckled. "I think it's swimming in my veins now."

Kathryn smiled. "It's a favorite this time of the year. The two men who were here last night…," she waited for George to nod his acknowledgment, "they bring a box of hot chocolate mix every year. It's everyone's favorite, but we get so excited, we go through it in about a week!"

Taking the last swallow of his drink, George set his mug down and picked up a cookie. "These are really good."

Kathryn smiled.

"No, really, I ate the entire plate you gave me before I got here the other night and I thought at the time you should be baking for a living instead of working for me."

"George, I like working for you. At least, most of the time."

"I can't imagine why," George said in between bites of his chocolate chip cookie.

"You're a good businessman, George." Kathryn turned and tucked her feet underneath her legs, cross-legged, and faced George. "I admire your success and I'm glad to be a part of it. You must realize my job is important to the family right now."

"I don't think I ever considered it before now."

Kathryn patted his arm. She couldn't resist touching him somehow. "No reason why you should. I realized today that I don't know much about you away from work. I mean, I know James because he stops by occasionally, but I don't know about the rest of your family or what you do outside the office."

George turned sideways, bending his knee to rest on the cushion between them. "I don't have any other family besides James, Jenny, and John. I think I've been trying to convince myself I don't need anyone. It makes me feel as though I've wasted a lot of time.

All I've done is work."

"But you did have family."

"Yes," George looked up, into her eyes intensely, and swallowed, "I even had a girlfriend for a while, but that was a long time ago."

Kathryn was not interested in hearing about George's girlfriend, although she thought she should know what kind of girl attracted him. But not tonight. "Tell me about your mom."

"I don't remember much about her."

"Tell me about a special Christmas with your family."

"A special Christmas," George mused. "I'm not sure." Flickers of emotion passed over George's face and Kathryn sat still and waited. She desperately wanted to see him remember something good.

"Oh," George began, "Okay. I remember sitting in the kitchen while Mom baked cookies." George looked at the half-eaten cookie in his hand. "It must be why I love your cookies. They remind me of her."

He looked right into Kathryn's eyes and beyond the warmth and supple depth, she saw a vulnerability she'd never before seen. Without thinking, Kathryn reached for George's free hand and intertwined her fingers with his.

His glance at their interlocked fingers let her know he was aware of their connection, but he continued, "We were laughing and talking and trying to see who could make the biggest cookie. She had the most wonderful laugh, my mom." A cloud of sadness covered his eyes for a moment.

"George," Kathryn interjected, "I don't want to bring up memories that make you sad. You don't have to go on if you don't want to."

"No, it's okay, Kathryn." George loosened his grip on her hand, but continued to play with her fingers. "I think before I would have said I didn't have any good memories of my family."

"Really?"

"But maybe I blocked them out, you know, because I couldn't stand the idea of not just losing them when they died, but losing a good life."

"Oh, George."

George shared more about his parents and his sister, Adele, than

Kathryn ever expected. Stories of them working together and playing together made the tragedy of his parents' accident that much more painful and Kathryn's heart bled a little for the little boy sent away to boarding school and abandoned by his grandparents. She was even a little angry at Adele for not sticking up for her brother and only worrying about her own escape from the cold, stern grandfather.

"But George," Kathryn protested, "why didn't Adele plead your cause and make them at least keep you at home?"

"It's okay, Kathryn," George smiled. "We were all going through our own stage of grief. I ran across my granddad's journals recently," George paused, as though a light suddenly turned on in a dark room, "and I can't hold it against him anymore. I did for a long time. I think I had convinced myself I hated him for what he did. But after reading his final entries, I saw him for what he really was. A lonely, sad, grieving old man who turned to the only thing he knew—his work—and shut out everything else, even my grandma."

Kathryn let go of George's hand and reached around his shoulders, holding him in a tight hug. She felt his arms slowly come around her back and match her hold and the rightness of being in his arms nearly overwhelmed her. Kathryn's muffled wishes whispered aloud, "I wish I could turn back the clock and change everything for you. I wish I could help you and show you that there's good in the world and even though our loved ones are taken from us, there's a promise to be with them again. I wish I could help you find that happiness you had as a child."

21

Happiness. In all the time he had spent with Kathryn at her parents' home in the last two days, that was the word he could use to describe the atmosphere. Happiness had never been so tangible. And sitting here, awkwardly holding Kathryn in his arms, brought on such a thrill of happiness, George was undone.

He slowly stood, bringing Kathryn with him. He wasn't ready to let go yet. Had anyone ever felt so right? She fit him. Her arms were wound around his waist, her head resting on his chest. He peeked down his nose and saw her eyes were closed, but her arms were firm.

He hadn't planned to tell her about his granddad's journals, but trusting Kathryn was something he had done for so long, he knew it was right.

Yet standing there, he was still blown away at having her in his arms. His heart had been heavy when they talked about his family. But the more he told her the stories of his youth, the lighter he felt. And now, holding each other, the stuffy grayness that had shrouded him for so many years melted fully away. The final chips of ice were gone.

"I don't need the happiness of a child, Kathryn," he said. *I only need you.* The words came as a surprise, but remained silent. His heart reached a steady, constant beat as he held this woman who eased his soul, bore poverty and heartbreak with grace and faith, and George knew his life would never be the same.

Time stood still as he kept Kathryn in the safety of his arms. He felt her shiver slightly and wondered if she shared the tingles and spark he experienced while they embraced.

"Kathryn," George whispered.

"Hmmm?"

Kathryn's voice floated through his mind, dancing around his heart, touching and tingling until he needed more.

"Kathryn," George repeated.

Kathryn relaxed her hold around his waist and leaned back slightly, still tangled, still wrapped in his arms, but with room to look up into his face.

Her sleepy, warm eyes pooled like a high mountain lake and George fell in like a cliff diver. Kathryn's lips parted, caught in the moment as George leaned closer. He felt rather than heard her quick intake of breath.

"Kathryn," George said once again, although he knew he had her attention now. "It's later."

Her deep, husky voice stirred George's soul. "So, it is. George, please kiss me."

When his mouth lowered to hers, it was as if the world exploded into thousands of spiraling twinkle lights. Softly, tenderly at first, he drank of her sweetness as she responded in kind, winding her arms around his neck and pulling him closer still.

Sheer perfection melted into George's arms. He angled his mouth over hers and drank deeper, over and over again.

"Oh, George," Kathryn breathed, when they came up for air.

Shaking from the emotional enormity of the step that led to that earth-shattering kiss and rubbing up and down Kathryn's arms at the same time, George took a couple of deep breaths to get his bearings.

"I...uh...I think we'd better call it a night, Kathryn," he said.

The huskiness of his voice seemed to reverberate through Kathryn's back as he continued to hold on.

"I...I...you...you...uh, yeah, we should get some sleep. I'll see you in the morning." George released Kathryn's arms and stepped back, instantly chilled. Now she was too far away. He stepped forward, but Kathryn stepped back and George stopped.

"I think you're right, George," Kathryn agreed, touching her puffy lips with her delicate fingertips, lips George had kissed so thoroughly. "We should get some sleep. Good night, George, and Merry Christmas."

George hadn't moved, so Kathryn turned him around and gently nudged him in the direction of the kitchen. He followed her lead and before he could regroup, he found himself sitting on the little bed in the back-pantry bedroom, wondering how his life had changed so dramatically and what he had to do to kiss Kathryn again. Sleep? How in the world would he ever fall asleep after her life-altering kisses?

Sliding under the thin blanket, George lay on his back with his hands crossed behind his head and relived each kiss as wave after wave of warmth and goodness crashed over him. Slowly the warmth no longer crashed, but drowned him completely and he closed his eyes.

A thin light illuminated the park gate and George walked with purpose. The gate had been left ajar, but no one seemed to be standing guard. As George entered, he felt his hand being taken by a small child.

Looking down, he thought for sure he recognized the child, but couldn't give her a name. She didn't speak. In fact, George didn't speak either, but followed the pull of the little girl's hand as she led him deeper into the park.

The path was solid beneath George's feet, but he noticed it wasn't made from asphalt, like the park paths near his home, or from dirt, like the hiking trails he remembered as a boy.

The edges of the park blurred into a dimness that made it necessary for George to focus only on the little girl and what was immediately in front of them.

George could see on the edges of his vision others walking along the same path, but he couldn't see their faces. Some were alone. Some were with one or two other people. Those that were alone seemed to be looking for others. He looked down at the little girl. Her sweet smile and angelic face calmed him and he squeezed her hand. Her eyes grew bigger and she squeezed back, but the half smile and peaceful expression on her face never altered.

Suddenly they stopped in front of a lone man, sitting on a bench along the path. George knew this man. His pained countenance hid well his youthful looks.

"Geoff McAllister." George stated his name quietly.

Geoff looked at George and tears welled up in his eyes. He mouthed the word 'no,' and bent his head over into his waiting hands. His shoulders shook with sobs.

George stepped back. Geoff never showed emotion. He had never looked back when they pushed forward in their business. Determined beyond measure, Geoff had taken every opportunity, stepped on every toe in the way, and cut every corner to get ahead. At the time George had envied Geoff's cutthroat approach. But seeing Geoff so miserable and alone, he thought back on the number of people hurt by Geoff's actions. He no longer wanted to even remotely resemble his former partner.

A pull to his sleeve found him once again on the path through the park, now a brilliant flowering garden, with paths leading away into grassy areas populated with small groups. The melancholy mood from seeing Geoff slowly dematerialized as George stood on the edge of the grass and gazed wonderingly at people he knew, oh, so well.

His mother, father, grandmother and grandfather, along with his sister, Adele, all sat on a large blanket laughing and eating a picnic lunch. He raised his hand to get their attention, but they didn't see him. He tried to walk closer to their circle in the grass, but his legs wouldn't budge. Poised to move, but stuck, all he could do was watch as they interacted with each other. George couldn't hear what they said, but laughter filled their faces and his heart lifted.

He longed to speak with them. He didn't understand why he could see them, but they couldn't see him. Why couldn't he join them?

Another tug on his sleeve and his family seemed to melt away into the mist. Once again, he was walking along the path, now searching the others along the way for someone he might know.

As he approached a woman with long, dark hair, he was reminded of Kathryn. From the back, he could almost swear it was her. But as he and his companion caught up with the woman, he instantly recognized not Kathryn, but Elizabeth, Kathryn's sister.

The serene look on her face calmed him. She knew no pain. She knew no sorrow. Yet she was not smiling and George could feel her yearning for the life she had known, even though it had brought her both pain and sorrow. Her eyes were clear and bright, a mirror of Kathryn's except they were a bluer green. All George could think of was her children who no longer could talk to her, sit with her, or sing with her. It would be ages before she would have them with her again.

Did it have to be this way? What was the purpose of putting him in her path if not to prevent this awful thing from happening? He could no longer prevent any of the others from moving on to the next life, but he could do something for Elizabeth!

"No!" George shouted.

The image disappeared as though a light had turned off and George found himself gasping for air as he sat up in the little bed.

Taking deep breaths to regain control of his erratic heartbeat, he closed his eyes and captured a tiny vision of what he must do. Exhausted from the onslaught of his dream, George fell back onto the pillow. Before he understood what he was doing, he slipped from the bed onto his knees and, for the first time in a long time, prayed for guidance. Peace washed through George and as he once again reclaimed the little bed, he began formulating his plans.

22

The sound of a delighted squeal pierced the air and George smiled. Dressing in a hurry, he neatly folded Justin's jeans and flannel shirt and left them on the little bed. He would be forever grateful for Justin's generosity. Dressed once again in his suit slacks and dress shirt felt strange after the past two days living in a Christmas dream. Still, they promised they would dig him out today and he certainly couldn't stay here, even though he couldn't think of anywhere else he'd rather be. Well, he could think of being anywhere else as long as he was with Kathryn. It wasn't the house that clicked his life into place, it was her.

Leaving the little bedroom with a soft salute and whispered prayer of thanks, he casually made his way through the kitchen and stood on the brink of the living room, anticipating the scene to come.

Kathryn sat on the sofa crossed-legged, much as she had last night and the power of remembering her in his arms only hours ago, of her lips trembling beneath his, nearly buckled his knees. Using the wall to brace himself as the image floated away, he turned to the imps emitting the squeals that initially brought him to the living room. Maggie and Caroline danced around the Christmas tree, holding presents high in the air and singing strains of something, but really nothing at all. Tommy huddled in the corner, savoring whatever he had discovered in the open box, surrounded by shreds of Christmas wrapping.

"My turn!" shouted Maggie.

"And then, my turn!" Caroline echoed.

Maggie sat on the floor and began the harrowing chore of opening her present. It seemed as though she was trying to make time stand still by moving as slowly as possible.

"Oh, Maggie," Kathryn teased. "Stop stalling. You're making me crazy!"

Giggles were her only answer, along with a bass-toned chuckle.

Kathryn gasped. "George!"

"Merry Christmas, Kathryn."

The sparkle in her emerald eyes eclipsed his own and he soaked in her gaze.

"Merry Christmas, George," Kathryn breathed.

George saw Elizabeth, who was sitting by the window on the side of the Christmas tree, give a pointed look to Justin, who was on the floor at her feet. George didn't care who knew at this point. Hiding his feelings went against his new resolve.

"Merry Christmas, everyone." George said to the room, still with his eyes on Kathryn.

"Merry Christmas, George," the chorus answered.

Kathryn jumped up and rushed to the tree, whispering something in Elizabeth's ear before reaching for a small package in Christmas wrapping. She held the box out for George.

"This is for you, George," Kathryn smiled, "from Santa."

"From Santa, eh?"

"He dropped it by last night, after you were all snug in your bed."

"With visions of sugar plums dancing in my head?"

"Is that what was dancing in your head, George?" Kathryn asked with a knowing smile.

He couldn't very well tell the entire room he had thought of very little else but her deliciously sweet kisses most of the night. So, he let his eyes tell the story only to her and simply stated, "Of course."

"Come, sit down," Kathryn invited and George carefully stepped around Maggie and Caroline, who were cooing over their opened gifts, before sitting snugly next to Kathryn.

George slowly opened his present. As much as he had silently chided Maggie for going so slow, he understood the desire to relish every moment and make it last as long as possible. Kathryn's zing of energy as she sat on the edge of the sofa, watching every movement of his fingers as he sliced through the tape and extricated a small box, shot through George like a laser. Did everyone sense the sparks zipping back and forth between them?

"Come on, George," Kathryn said impatiently, "you're as bad as the little kids."

"You're going to pay for that remark, Kathryn,"

"Oh, I'll pay. Don't you worry."

"Kathryn!" Mary said.

Mary's voice startled George and he quickly unpacked his gift from the tissue inside the box. A miniature snow globe was fitted with a three-tiered snowman standing proudly inside. George shook the snow globe and soft, shimmering white snow floated through the air surrounding the snowman.

"It's perfect."

"It's so you'll always remember spending Christmas with us."

"You think I'll forget?"

"Well," Kathryn's face flushed and she pushed her hand against her mouth. "No," came the muffled reply.

George tucked the snow globe back into its box and tipped Kathryn's chin up so she would look into his eyes.

"Thank you," he said as his lips brushed hers ever so lightly.

Maggie stood up and placed her hands on her hips, staring at George. "Why are you thanking Aunt Katie? Your present was from Santa."

George swallowed quickly, "Oh, well, I was thanking her for letting Santa know where to find me."

Kathryn buried her face in her lap, shaking with laughter.

Appeased, Maggie turned back to her toy.

George could hear Elizabeth's chuckle behind him.

Later, George and Kathryn stood at the kitchen sink, peeling potatoes and talking.

Every story Kathryn told about growing up in this loving family made George's heart long for a family of his own. Never had the yearning been so strong, never had he been so desperate to fix the wrongs he had done, even if the wrongs were simply oversights or omissions of generosity.

George found ways to touch Kathryn, leaning over her to reach a dish towel, brushing up against her arm while they laughed over another story about Maggie and Caroline, touching her shoulder while he put away a dish on a shelf above her head.

"George!"

"What?"

"You're driving me nuts."

"What?"

"I can't stand all this almost touching."

"What do you want me to do, ravish you here in the kitchen?"

"Of course not. Come with me."

Kathryn grabbed his hand and they slipped just inside the back-pantry bedroom.

"And this is a good idea because…"

"Oh George, just kiss me."

Kathryn answered his kiss with a passion George had only dreamed about last night. Breathless and bewitched, George came up for air. "Kathryn, are you trying to get me into trouble?"

"Trouble?"

"What if your father came in here?"

"Oh," Kathryn said as she sucked air to catch her breath.

"Look, honey," George said, "I'd like to spend the rest of the day doing nothing but kissing you, well, at least, I mean, I…I want to kiss you in the worst way, but…"

Kathryn threw herself into George's arms and hugged on tight. George wrapped his arms around her and they just stood there for at least an eternity. The way her body fit to his and the smell of her apple cinnamon shampoo heated George until he was sure they would spontaneously combust.

"Kathryn, honey," George mumbled through her curls, "you're killing me. Let's go finish the potatoes."

23

Kathryn sighed as she leaned against the doorway between the kitchen and living room. George would be leaving soon, going back to his house in the city and leaving her here. The entire holiday seemed like a dream from a Hallmark movie and she wondered if it would all disappear when they returned to their normal lives. If that happened, Kathryn would have to find another job. There was no way she could work with George now if he went back to being a bad-tempered stranger.

They were outside now, George, Justin, and her father, digging George's car out of the snow. She could see them talking and laughing as they shoveled the snow. Soon, too soon, George would be unstuck and gone. Kathryn's heart heaved.

It wasn't as though she wanted to keep him a prisoner. She just didn't know if two days in the snow and her parents' humble home could change years of seclusion and unhappiness.

Well, she wasn't going to let him go without a fight! Kathryn pulled her coat from the closet and stomped into her snow boots. She was going to spend every moment she could with him right up to the minute he drove away.

Kathryn tried to appear nonchalant as she walked up beside George.

"Hey, gorgeous," George said easily.

"I came to make sure you were doing it right."

Justin laughed. "Of course, you were."

Kathryn blushed.

George shoulder bumped her. "We're almost there."

Justin hooked up the chain from his Suburban, gave George a 'thumbs up' sign, and went to climb into the vehicle.

With George and Henry on the back end pushing and Justin carefully pulling with the car, the sad, cold Volvo was gently rocked out of its nest in the ditch and slowly climbed back onto the driveway. George brushed the snow off the windows and hood and opened the driver's door. Leaving the door open, he reached in and slid the key into the ignition, turning the motor over. Reluctant at first, the Volvo sprung to life after only a little coaxing and George gave the steering wheel a little pat. "Good job," he said.

Scrambling out of the car with it still running, George walked up to Justin. "Thanks, man, I really appreciate your help."

"No problem."

George turned to Henry and Kathryn watched the three men she admired most in the world shake hands with gratitude. Henry beamed. Kathryn knew that helping people kept her dad going, gave him purpose, and reminded him daily of his blessings.

Checking around George's car, Kathryn noticed only a small dent in the passenger fender.

"Not too much damage." George was so close she could feel his breath on her face.

"Not at all," she agreed. "You were expecting more?"

"I almost expected the car to be totaled."

"Why?"

"I don't know. I guess I thought it had to be something terribly destructive to keep me here for two days."

"It wasn't the car. It was the weather."

"It wasn't the weather. It was the people."

"You were our prisoner, weren't you?" Kathryn chuckled as she tried to figure out what she heard in George's voice.

"I wish I still could be. I don't ever want to leave."

Kathryn's breath hiccupped.

"But you know, I must." George shook his head sadly. "And I can't ask you to come with me because you need to spend this time with your family."

"I'll be there next Monday."

"If I asked you to come in this Friday, would you?"

"Friday?"

"I thought maybe I could take you out for dinner on Friday and then out for New Year's Eve on Saturday."

"I think I'd like that."

"Good. I think I can leave now, knowing you're going to be there at the end of this week."

Justin and Henry had gone back inside the house as George and Kathryn talked, but George needed to say goodbye. He quickly turned off the car and Kathryn walked him back to the house.

Everyone gathered in the living room. George took off the heavy winter coat Justin had loaned him over the weekend and handed it to Kathryn. She hung it up in the closet by the front door and came back with George's suit coat. Once he pulled it on over his dress shirt, he looked very much like the man he was when he arrived two days ago, and Kathryn started to worry again.

Standing by the door, Kathryn waited for George to say goodbye to the children first, then Justin and Elizabeth. When he came to Henry and Mary, he asked if they could talk together for a minute in private.

Henry and Mary led George down the hall to one of the bedrooms.

"What's that all about?" Elizabeth asked the moment the bedroom door was closed.

Kathryn was as bewildered as Ellie. "I have no idea."

"He's not, like, asking for your hand in marriage, is he?"

"Of course not." Right? Kathryn's heart quaked. It had really been only two days. Two days since he had gone from the world's worst sourpuss to her happy heartthrob?

"Well, what else could it be?"

"Just stop."

"But..."

"Stop."

Justin cleared his throat. "He seems like a really great guy, Kathryn. I don't understand all the stories you used to tell about him being such a beast."

"He's really changed."

"Maybe he was there all the time, but it took being stranded out here to let himself go."

"Maybe. He wants to take me out on the weekend."

"So, it's not temporary."

"I guess not. Oh, Ellie, I'm nervous."

"Nervous?"

Kathryn swallowed and checked down the hall to make sure the door was still closed between her and her parents and George. "I've been in love with him for a long time, Ellie. I know I told stories about him being mean, but all that time I was hoping beyond hope there was a good man inside and every once in a while, there was this glimmer of something, something he tried so hard to hide and I knew if I could only chip away at the stone, the real man would be released."

Ellie pulled her wheelchair up to Kathryn and squeezed her hand. "I think he's quite taken with you, too."

"Yeah?"

The door to the bedroom down the hall opened and George strode out, his face resolved and serious. Kathryn felt a rock land squarely in her stomach. Oh, dear.

"Walk me to my car, Kathryn?"

"Oh, sure," Kathryn said, zipping up her coat as George opened the door, saying goodbye again to everyone in the living room.

Once out the door, George gathered Kathryn's hand and pressed it around his arm.

"So, Friday night dinner and then Saturday, right? You'll be in the city by then?"

"I said I would."

George stopped by his car and pulled Kathryn into a tight embrace. "How will I manage until then?"

"I'm sure you'll be fine, George. What did you talk to my parents about?"

"It's a secret. I know I'll be fine, but I'll miss you."

"I'm not sure the beginning of our relationship should include secrets, George."

George chuckled. "Don't worry. You'll know soon enough. You bring out the best in me Kathryn. Thank you."

"Thank you? For what?"

George slipped his hands behind her neck. Pulling her close, he kissed her long and thoroughly, as though this kiss had to last a long time. Because it did, she thought. Friday was forever away.

"I'll see you Friday. Come to the office."

"Okay. Drive safe."

After George drove away, Kathryn stood in the snow for several long minutes wondering if Friday would bring back the old George and if the magic only lasted as long as Christmas.

24

The cold, sterile dimness that assaulted George when he entered his ancestral home nearly knocked him over. Certainly, the comparison between Henry and Mary's home filled with Christmas and love and this barren building which was truly only filled with sadness and remorse should be in itself enough to stand out in George's mind and heart that he needed to make changes.

George couldn't believe the difference he felt after experiencing Christmas with the Gleasons and, of course, after kissing Kathryn. Would it all mystically dematerialize as quickly as it had magically appeared? George sat down in the chair in the library where he had read the journals of his granddad and picked up the journal again. Jacob Stone's last words seeped into George's soul as he contemplated the changes he was making.

I've been thinking over these last few weeks of all the times I've passed over the opportunity to be kind or forgiving or gentle toward my family.

George thought of James, Jenny and Adele's husband, John. They were the only family he had left. Cringing at the memory of his last meeting with James, how he practically threw him out of his office when he had only stopped by to say Merry Christmas. Of course, he had thrown George under the bus when Mr. Hardy asked about a donation. But now, George wished he had donated. Determined to right the wrongs in his life, he made a mental note to find Mr. Hardy and make a donation that would make up for not only this year, but a lot of lost time.

How will I face a God I scorned and neglected in life?

George thought of the candlelight service on Christmas Eve. The story of Christ's birth resonated deep and he almost ached with a need to find out more. He was convinced Kathryn would help him find the answers he looked for.

I hope George will find happiness with Elaine and not allow his business to become his mistress.

George felt bad about his failed relationship with Elaine because he had done exactly what his granddad had hoped he wouldn't. He knew Elaine had moved on and found someone to love, someone who loved her. The joy and happiness he experienced with Kathryn over the last few days were so much more than he ever felt with Elaine, he knew it was better that their relationship had failed. He never would have found his way to this point with Elaine. Kathryn's beautiful face filled his mind's eye and he sat back, deep into the cushion of the chair and closed his eyes to the room, but feasted on the mental vision of Kathryn's face.

The hall clock chimed the hour. George quickly stood and made his way to his office. It was time to put his plans in motion. Picking up the phone, he dialed James' phone number.

"Merry Christmas!" James lighthearted voice called into the phone.

"Merry Christmas, James," said George. He waited while James figured out who was calling.

"Uncle George?" came the tentative reply.

"Yes. I called to wish you and Jenny a very Merry Christmas. Oh, and to see if you both would like to share dinner with me here at the house tomorrow evening."

Silence.

George waited.

Still silence.

"Uh, James?" George asked, worried now that James might have fainted and was passed out on the floor.

"Who is this really? Is this some kind of joke?"

James sounded indignant and it made George smile, but he shook his head with dismay. He had a lot of ground to make up. "It's not a joke, James. I know it doesn't sound like me, but I've made some decisions and I'm making changes in my life. One of those changes involves you. I would like you and your lovely wife to come to dinner tomorrow."

"Uh huh."

George plowed through James' stupor. "I'll have to bring in take-out because I haven't had time to hire a housekeeper yet, but shall we say about 7:00?"

"Uh huh."

George snickered. "I'll call you tomorrow make sure we're still on, okay?"

"Uh huh."

"Okay, then, goodbye James and please tell Jenny I said Merry Christmas. See you tomorrow at seven."

"Uncle George?" James' voice was weak and leery.

"Yes?"

"You're okay, right? You're not dying or anything, are you?"

"I certainly hope not." George said, chuckling and thinking about all the plans he was making for Kathryn to become part of his life.

"Okay. See you tomorrow."

After hanging up the phone, George smiled and was glad James had pulled out of his fog even that much before the end of the call.

George returned to his favorite chair in the library and closed his grandfather's journals.

"I'm not going to become like you, Granddad," he said aloud to the book. "I've seen what it did to you and to Geoff McAllister and I don't want that for my life." George continued to speak out in the cold room, "I'm going to change my ways starting today, starting now."

He took long steps to the full-length windows which ran along the south wall of the room and pulled the drapes open. Brilliant winter sunlight flooded the room and George coughed slightly from the disturbance of dust mites hiding in the drapes. Already the room felt better.

Moving from room to room, he felt as though someone had

finally released him from jail. Whipping open curtain after curtain, the light poured into the house. Even in the late afternoon, the sense of gloom that had previously permeated the entire house fled and George knew it wasn't just the house. It was him.

Arriving at work early the next morning, George was grateful for once in his life that the stores opened early the day after Christmas. He pulled the new Keurig machine from its box and set it up in the staff room. Once the machine was plugged in and filled with water, George followed the instructions to make sure it worked, then opened another box, this one full of assorted coffees and teas.

He put a separate box of assorted hot chocolate offerings on Kathryn's desk with a bow on top. George stopped and smiled. It was going to be a long week without her. He couldn't wait until she saw the transformation.

A knock at the door grabbed his attention and he headed for the front of the office. Greeting the delivery man with a spirited "Merry Christmas," he motioned for him to enter. Twenty-five 4-inch poinsettias filled the cart the man pulled into the room. George quickly helped him remove the plants from the cart, tipped him generously and with another wish of Merry Christmas and Happy New Year, sent him on his way. The clock on the wall let him know he still had fifteen minutes before his staff would arrive.

Placing the holiday flowers on each desk, he surveyed his simple handiwork before retreating into his office. He left the door ajar and waited with a silly grin on his face.

Sounds of 'oohs' and 'aahs' warmed George's soul as his employees walked in the door of the office and found the surprises on their desks. Exclamations of 'look at that' and 'this is so nice' mingled with giggles and cheers.

When George opened his door, everyone froze. Fighting the urge to fall back into his old persona, he allowed himself to smile at his employees.

George cleared his throat. "Good morning."

A chorus of good mornings replied.

"I, uh, want to, uh…" George closed his eyes briefly and wished Kathryn was here to stand beside him. He cleared his throat again. "I want to wish you all Merry Christmas!"

"Merry Christmas," echoed back.

He motioned to everyone to step closer. "I've been re-thinking some of our office policies and you'll find a new coffee machine in the staff room with a selection of coffees and teas. I'll also be contacting the bakery down the street and there will be pastries every Tuesday from now on in time for the weekly staff meeting. The poinsettias are my gift to you and you can keep them here in the office or take them home."

George almost laughed at the stunned looks on everyone's face. "I also wanted to let you know that you are now free to decorate your desks with family pictures or whatever you would like. Well, within reason. Please keep it professional."

Murmurs of delight filtered back to George.

Stacy Cunningham, his head bookkeeper, tentatively took a step forward of the crowd. "Mr. Stone," she began, "is Kathryn coming back?" Her wringing hands spoke volumes.

George couldn't stop the smile on his face. "Yes, she's just spending some time with her family. She'll be in on Friday."

A general sigh could be felt more than heard and George wondered what they would make of his new relationship with his executive assistant.

"Okay, everyone," he said with a smile. "Let's get to work."

The crowd dispersed, each one to their own cubicle and George wondered about lowering the cubicle walls so the room was more open and people could actually see each other instead of feeling isolated in their little rooms. He made a mental note to ask Kathryn when she returned.

Once back in his office, he booted up his computer. It was time to find a housekeeper and get ready for his future.

Just before lunch, with plans firmly in place, interviews for housekeepers scheduled for that afternoon, Stacy popped her head through the doorway to let him know he had a call.

"It's Henry Gleason," she said with some anxiousness in her voice. "I hope Kathryn's okay."

"Thanks, Stacy," George waved her away. "I'm sure she's just fine."

George re-situated himself in his chair, pulled on his collar and straightened his tie before picking up the handset of his phone. Swallowing hard, he said into the phone, "Henry. What can you tell me?"

Epilogue

"**O**kay, everybody. She's almost here!" Kathryn dropped her phone in her pocket and smoothed down her red, white and blue top celebrating the 4th of July and the reason for the picnic today. Well, that was the reason they gave Ellie. She had no idea the party was really for her and a special surprise Kathryn was saving for her new husband.

George slipped his arms around her waist from behind and nuzzled her ear. His whispers of how he wanted to occupy her time later sent shivers down her spine and a blush to her cheeks.

Kathryn giggled. "Later."

George chuckled and let her go with a nibble to her neck.

"I never thought married life would include 'later' as much as it does."

"Come on," Kathryn said, faking an indignant voice. "You are hardly a deprived husband."

George snickered.

Fortunately, Jenny chose that moment to interrupt and George mumbled something about checking on the grill as he left Kathryn's side.

"I'm sorry for interrupting." Jenny said warily.

"You've got to get over being timid of George, Jenny," Kathryn patted her arm. "He's a big blowhard sometimes, but he's really a sweetheart."

"I know," Jenny agreed. "I just can't seem to let go of the way he treated Jimmy and me for so long."

"Well, after today, I think you'll be able to look forward instead of looking back."

"I hope so."

"You know," Kathryn admitted, "I was nervous around him, too, even up until the day he proposed."

"Really?" Jenny's look showed her intrigue. "I never heard about how he proposed from your point of view, you know, just what he told Jimmy."

"It was Christmas magic." Kathryn sighed.

Jenny's tiny laugh stopped Kathryn's daydream.

"It really was." Kathryn was suddenly quite sober and looked at Jenny intently. "You know he was trapped at my parents' over Christmas last year."

Jenny nodded.

"Well, he asked me to come to work that Friday, even though I was still on vacation. The time we spent together over Christmas was like a dream come true and I decided it was better to find out the dream was over earlier than later, so I went into work that afternoon."

"But I thought he proposed on New Year's Eve."

"Oh, he did, but he asked me to come to the office on Friday to take me out for dinner. I think he just wanted to see me." Kathryn giggled.

Jenny's attention was riveted.

"Anyway, I went into the office and everyone's desk displayed a beautiful poinsettia and he had bought a coffee machine—a really nice one—for the staff room as well as a huge assortment of coffees and teas. And," she leaned in toward Jenny as though she held a great secret, "he gave me my very own box of assorted hot chocolate for the coffee machine."

Jenny smiled.

"So, you have to understand that before he spent Christmas with my family, he didn't allow anyone to have any kind of decoration on their desk. It was all business and he was a tightwad to say the least. We kept asking for a coffee machine, but he always said no."

"But that doesn't have anything to do with asking you to marry him."

"No," Kathryn agreed, "but I think he was buttering me up. Anyway, he told me he was taking me shopping the next day for a year-end bonus present."

Jenny's eyes widened.

"Oh, I knew what he was doing," Kathryn assured her. "He only called it that because he was afraid I would say no. I think he was just as worried that the time at my parents' house was imaginary and he didn't think I would go along with the shopping trip."

"It's so romantic."

"Which is my point, Jenny. George didn't have a romantic bone in his body until that Christmas. It was truly magical."

"So how did he propose?"

"Well, we went shopping and he took me to so many stores my head was swimming, but we finally found the perfect dress, shoes, and handbag. Then, when he came to pick me up for our late dinner that night, he brought me a gorgeous mink coat."

"Oh!"

"Oh, yes. I was flabbergasted. And before I knew it, he slipped the coat over my shoulders and was pushing me out the door."

"Oh, wow."

"Yes, well, I didn't know quite what to think and I was starting to worry that the gifts were too much and he would expect something in return I wasn't prepared to offer, if you know what I mean."

"I didn't think George was like that," Jenny said.

"I know. It was totally against everything I knew about him, but, you know, you just worry at that point."

"So, then what?"

"So, we went to the top of the Regency Hotel, you know, the Calabria Restaurant. It was beautifully decorated for the holidays and I felt like a princess walking in wearing my new mink coat. Especially with such a handsome man on my arm."

"Of course," Jenny said, "he's not as handsome as my Jimmy."

"Oh, of course," Kathryn agreed with a wink. "We had a lovely dinner and when it was over, George suggested we take a walk along the river."

"Nice, but cold."

"Yes, well, I had on this fur coat so I was warm enough."

"Then what?" Jenny's eyes grew wider.

Kathryn giggled. "So then, as we walked, he held my hand. Then he started kissing my fingers and I was getting these little tingles all up my arm."

"Oooo."

"He took me over to a wall of lights that was surrounded by a row of trees, all lit up with colored Christmas lights. He told me he was a little cold and I let him wrap his arms around my waist inside my coat and I wrapped my coat around his shoulders. We stood there, looking into each other's eyes and he said..." Kathryn paused.

"He said what?" Jenny asked breathlessly.

"He said, 'Kathryn, I'm a new man because of you. You've shown me the beauty of living and the joy of the season. I can't live without you. I'll love you for forever and I hope you'll consent to be my wife.'"

"Oh, that's so amazing."

"Then he took my ring from his pocket and asked me, officially, to marry him."

"And you said yes."

"Obviously," Kathryn chuckled.

"I hope you've written down that story so you can tell your children one day."

"Oh, don't worry. I started a new journal on Christmas day. I had a feeling that Christmas was the beginning of my new life."

The cacophony that accompanies young children started out low and then started to grow as Maggie, Caroline, and Tommy all came around the corner of the house toward the backyard. Kathryn smiled her biggest smile. Relating her story of George's proposal brought back the dreamlike quality of her life since Christmas. Sometimes she needed to pinch herself just to make sure it was real.

Maggie ran up and tackled George around the legs. He leaned over and hefted her up into the air, catching her on the way down and hugging her tight. Kathryn knew he would always have a soft spot for Maggie.

Justin escorted Ellie around the corner and Kathryn felt the burn of happy tears at the back of her eyes. Seeing her sister walking with only the help of a cane after so many months in a wheelchair filled her heart with joy. And it was all because of George. If he had told her he was going to pay for Ellie's operation before they became engaged, she wasn't sure she could have said yes. She might have worried their love was tainted because of his incredible generosity.

He hadn't told anyone but her mom and dad, and asked them to make sure Ellie and Justin were okay with it first. They waited until just before Ellie's surgery before Kathryn found out it was all George's doing.

"Now that everyone's here," George began. "I have a little announcement."

Kathryn looked at George. She didn't have any idea what he was going to announce and she wondered if he had discovered her secret.

"I'm pleased to announce," George continued, "that Stone & McAllister is opening a west coast office at the end of this year. We are officially a national company."

A chorus of cheers surrounded their little group.

So much had transpired since the New Year and Kathryn knew about the expansion of the company. She just didn't realize George would announce it tonight. Breathing a sigh of relief, she smiled at the light applause and offers of congratulations for George.

George patted his hands in the air to quiet the welcome compliments. "And," George continued, "although James is completely qualified to open and run that office, I've decided to name him Vice President of our local office instead."

James' head shot up. "Really?"

"And hire a new VP for the new office," George concluded.

"I'm going to run your office here?" James asked, his voice a little unsteady.

"Are you ready?" George asked.

"You bet." James' grin almost reached his ears.

James had been working for George since the first of the year. His experience with his previous employer made him a perfect fit for George's office and had allowed Kathryn to stay home and make arrangements over the few short weeks before their March wedding. Since the wedding, she had been working on updating the house and bringing in the light. Making George's ancestral house into a truly loving home filled her heart with happiness. Seeing George excited about the little changes she was making brought them closer and the transformation in George, which began in her parents' humble home, continued to turn him into an amazingly generous and romantic man.

He couldn't seem to let go of Christmas, though. In fact, she often found sprigs of mistletoe hanging in strategic places just in time for George to sweep her off her feet with the most breathtaking kisses. She left each little sprig hanging where he placed it and now the house dripped with hanging berries and foliage. When he suggested they put up a Christmas tree in the living room window in June, she finally had to put her foot down and convince him to wait until December.

"I would like to propose a toast," Henry spoke over the crowd, lifting his glass of lemonade. A hush descended and all eyes were turned toward Henry. "To George, for his incredible generosity. We are so blessed to have him for a son."

George's eyes looked watery and he bent his head toward the ground. Kathryn sneaked up beside him and slipped her hand in his. He squeezed it tight.

"And to Ellie," Henry continued. "For a successful surgery and the fastest recovery on record."

"Yay!" shouted the children.

Tears ran down Ellie's cheeks and Justin knelt beside her and wiped them away. The gratitude in her eyes spoke volumes, thanks she had expressed to George personally many times.

Everyone smiled and Kathryn could tell George was glad to have the spotlight on someone else for a moment.

"Well," Kathryn said as the cheers quieted. "Since we're in the spirit of announcements," she paused, peeking through her eyelashes at her adorable husband, "I have a gift for George and I wanted all of you to be here for him to open it."

"This is an announcement?" George asked.

George's eyebrows raised as she winked at him. She grabbed a gift bag that had been quietly waiting beneath the patio table for this very moment.

"Merry Christmas, George," Kathryn said with a grin.

"Uh, Kathryn, it's not Christmas. I've tried to convince you we should celebrate Christmas all year and you keep telling me I have to wait until December." The teasing in his eyes were for her alone and she could sense everyone holding their breath for her response.

"Don't worry," she assured him and directed her attention to the watching crowd. Even the children stood totally still as they looked at their Uncle George. "You'll understand when you open it."

George reached into the gift bag and pulled out a small bundle wrapped in white tissue paper. Carefully unwrapping the paper layer by layer, he exposed an ornate glass Christmas tree ornament depicting a smiling baby sitting in a sleigh full of Christmas presents. At the bottom of the sleigh were the words "Baby's 1st Christmas."

Visibly shaken, George carefully set the delicate ornament on the patio table and turned to Kathryn, taking her hands in his. "A baby for Christmas?"

Kathryn nodded. "I know we've teased you about being Father Christmas since January. But I think I like 'Daddy' better."

George pulled her into his arms and kissed her good and proper and quite thoroughly, until his forgotten audience started clapping.

"We'll continue this later," he whispered in her ear.

"Later," Kathryn agreed. She could hardly wait.

The End

THANKS

Every book is a work of love and I loved writing this adaptation of *A Christmas Carol* by Charles Dickens. George and Kathryn's story presented itself to me one year when the Christmas season was coming to a close. Adapting an existing and well-loved novel is a gratifying, but tricky business. I will always enjoy the original story, but I loved turning Scrooge into someone we could all sigh over, too.

Thank you for taking time to read *The Spirit of Christmas* and may you have the true holiday spirit in your life all through the year.

The best way to help authors is to write a review. If you have the time, I would truly appreciate it! Amazon is best for me. Thanks!

I would love to hear from you. You can reach me at www.facebook.com/LaurainesBooks.

OTHER BOOKS BY LAURAINE HENDERSON

THE TRIPLE-DATE DARE

DAISIES IN THE DRIVEWAY

ROCK MY WORLD

THE COOKIE ROMANCE SERIES:
A COOKIE AND A KISS
A COOKIE AND A PROMISE
A COOKIE AND A SECRET (COMING SOON)

BUILDING A LIFE (COMING SOON)

NOTHING LEFT TO LOSE (RELEASE DATE: NOVEMBER 15, 2021)

Find out about these and other books in the works at
www.lauraine.henderson.com.

ABOUT THE AUTHOR

Lauraine Henderson began writing as a child, poems and journaling, until babies, building houses, and bookkeeping jobs usurped her world. Now, well established in the Oregon countryside and with the children grown, she devotes her spare time to writing. Besides being an avid reader, she enjoys painting with oils and watercolor, sewing, knitting, and making beaded jewelry.

Follow her on Facebook here: Facebook or Amazon here: Amazon

Made in the USA
Monee, IL
01 November 2021